mermaid Curse

The Black Pearl

LOUISE COOPER

PUFFIN

PUFFIN BOOKS

Published by the Penguin Group
Penguin Books Ltd, 80 Strand, London WC2R ORL, England
Penguin Group (USA) Inc., 375 Hudson Street, New York, New York 10014, USA
Penguin Group (Canada), 90 Eglinton Avenue East, Suite 700, Toronto, Ontario, Canada M4P 2Y3
(a division of Pearson Penguin Canada Inc.)
Penguin Ireland, 25 St Stephen's Green, Dublin 2, Ireland (a division of Penguin Books Ltd)
Penguin Group (Australia), 250 Camberwell Road, Camberwell, Victoria 3124, Australia
(a division of Pearson Australia Group Pty Ltd)
Penguin Books India Pvt Ltd, 11 Community Centre, Panchsheel Park, New Delhi – 110 017, India
Penguin Group (NZ), 67 Apollo Drive, Rosedale, North Shore 0632, New Zealand
(a division of Pearson New Zealand Ltd)
Penguin Books (South Africa) (Pty) Ltd, 24 Sturdee Avenue, Rosebank,
Johannesburg 2196, South Africa

Penguin Books Ltd, Registered Offices: 80 Strand, London WC2R ORL, England

puffinbooks.com

First published 2008
2

Set in Sabon by Palimpsest Book Production Limited,
Grangemouth, Stirlingshire
Made and printed in England by Clays Ltd, St Ives plc

British Library Cataloguing in Publication Data
A CIP catalogue record for this book is available from the British Library

ISBN: 978-0-141-32226-1

www.greenpenguin.co.uk

Mixed Sources
Product group from well-managed
forests and other controlled sources
www.fsc.org Cert no. SA-COC-1592
© 1996 Forest Stewardship Council

Penguin Books is committed to a sustainable future
for our business, our readers and our planet.
The book in your hands is made from paper
certified by the Forest Stewardship Council.

*For Lucy and Tim – when they're old
enough to swim with the dolphins*

Prologue

Light shimmered in the undersea cave, casting all the colours of the rainbow across the walls and the surface of the huge still pool in the centre. On a rock couch draped with seaweed and decorated with hundreds of shells sat Taran, self-proclaimed mermaid Queen. She was very beautiful, but there was a cruel edge to her lovely face as she gazed at the golden circlet that she held in her hands. She turned her head and stared haughtily down at her servant.

'Well?' she said. 'What news have you brought?'

The servant, whose name was Tullor, hissed, 'Your Majesty, the rumour is true – Morvyr's long-lost daughter has returned!'

'Ah!' Taran clenched her fists and leaned towards him. 'And where is she now?'

'At this moment the girl is with her mother and brother in a cave not far from the place where the human fishermen live. But there's more, Your Majesty. The girl-child has the silver pearl. I saw it with my own eyes – and I heard it sing!'

Taran's cold green eyes lit up. 'This is far better than I expected! Well done, Tullor – I shall reward you! But first you must watch the girl, and follow her whenever you can. Make sure no one realizes what you are doing – especially those interfering dolphins!' Her face darkened in a scowl, then the scowl was replaced with a cunning smile. 'I have been patient for eleven years. I can be patient for a little while longer.' Her face twisted threateningly. 'Don't fail, Tullor. I want that pearl, I must have it – at any cost!'

When Tullor had gone, Taran looked again at the golden circlet in her hands. Seven pearls were set into the circlet, and the mermaid stroked them hungrily.

'Only seven,' she muttered to herself. 'Only seven. But soon I will have the eighth. Then there is only the black pearl to find – and when I have all nine, my power will be complete!'

Chapter One

It was going to be a perfect summer's day. Lizzy Baxter woke to the delightful sight of sunlight streaming in at her window, and the air in her bedroom felt warm and balmy. Throwing her duvet back, she scrambled out of bed and went to the window to peer out over the rooftops of the Cornish fishing port where she lived.

Beyond the roofs was the harbour, with the sea sparkling sapphire blue beyond. The morning bustle of the docks was in full swing, for several trawlers were due in on the tide and everything had to be ready

Lizzy could just see the boats in the bay, far out beyond the great landmark of St Michael's Mount, which shone in the brilliant early light. In less than an hour they would be home and unloading their catch.

Lizzy smiled to herself as she thought how much she already loved this place. It was hard to believe that she and her family had been living in Cornwall for only two weeks. So much had happened to her since they'd come to their new home . . . and it was all so astonishing and incredible that she could still hardly believe it was real.

Lizzy had always known that she and her older sister, Rose, weren't the Baxters' own children. Mr and Mrs Baxter had adopted Rose when she was one, and a few years later they had adopted Lizzy too. But, while they knew that Rose was an orphan, Lizzy's history was unknown. She had been found abandoned as a baby, not very far from here, and no one had been able to trace her family.

Lizzy had thought that she would never learn the truth about herself. But then Dad had been offered a lecturing post at a college in Cornwall, and the new house they bought was, by coincidence, in the same area where she had been found when she was small. Amid all the upheaval and excitement of moving, Lizzy hadn't had much time to wonder about her own past. But then one day on the nearby beach she had met a boy called Kes. And what she learned from him changed everything . . .

There were footsteps on the stairs and along the landing. Moments later Lizzy's door opened and Mrs Baxter's head appeared.

'Morning, love,' she said. 'Breakfast's nearly ready, so if you want a shower first you'd better get a move on.' She smiled. 'Another lovely day! We've been so lucky with the weather since we came. What are you doing – going to the beach again?'

'Mmm, yes, if that's all right?'

'Of course. Lucky you – I'm working, and Dad's going in to the college to be shown round. I don't know what Rose is up to; staying in bed half the morning, I expect, and then seeing Paul.'

Paul Treleaven was Rose's new boyfriend. His father was a fisherman and Paul sometimes went to sea with him. He was used to getting up early, but it hadn't rubbed off on Rose yet.

Lizzy grinned. 'I expect so too. OK, Mum, I'll be down in a few minutes.'

Mum went back downstairs and Lizzy headed for the bathroom. She showered quickly, then dashed back to her room, feeling light-hearted and excited. She had arranged to meet Kes today and she was so looking forward to seeing him again.

She pulled on a swimsuit, then put shorts and a T-shirt on top. As she wriggled the T-shirt over her head she suddenly remembered something. Her locket – it was on its silver chain round her neck. Quickly she unfastened the chain, and laid the locket on her bedside table. It was a very beautiful and unusual one, made from two pieces of mother-of-pearl. It had been with her when she was found as a baby, and she always wore it. But not when she went to the beach and the sea. Because now she knew the real truth about the locket. Inside it, hidden in a secret compartment, was a tiny treasure. And that treasure must be kept safe at all costs . . .

She gave the locket a last glance, then pushed her feet into flip-flops and hurried down to breakfast.

The trawlers that Lizzy had seen from her window were heading towards the harbour when one of the fishermen shouted to his crewmates and pointed further out to sea. A dolphin was heading westwards along the coast, streaking through the water. The fishermen watched it with smiles on their faces. They always enjoyed seeing dolphins. Sometimes the creatures came right up close, hoping to be thrown a few fish, and the men wondered if this one might follow them towards the harbour.

But the dolphin wasn't interested in fish. She had somewhere to go – and she needed to get there fast. Soon she had left the boats far behind and, as she surged on, the sun glinted on an unusual silver streak down the length of her back. Then suddenly she dived with hardly a splash, and swam down, down into the sea's depths. Ahead of her now was a forest of oar-weed, the long brown fronds swaying gently in the current. This was the right place . . . the dolphin plunged in among the weed, pushing herself through it with flicks of her powerful tail, and emerged on the far side, in front of an underwater cave. The cave entrance was covered by a waving curtain of finer weed, and many-coloured sea anemones grew around it.

The dolphin swam up to the entrance and gave a series of high, shrill whistles that echoed strangely through the water. She waited, and a few moments later the curtain parted and someone looked out.

'Arhans!' A boy emerged from the cave. He had black hair and brilliant blue eyes, and, though he looked completely human, he breathed underwater as easily as any ordinary boy did in air. He was smiling at the dolphin, delighted to see her, but as Arhans whistled again his expression changed.

'Mother? She's away in the forest, gathering food. Arhans, what is it? What's the matter?'

There was no mistaking the urgency in Arhans's shrill reply, and the boy, who had grown up understanding the language of dolphins, was alarmed. 'Yes, I'll take you to her – I know where she's gone, she shouldn't be hard to find. Come on!'

He dived into the forest, Arhans close on his heels. The boy was an expert swimmer, but the dolphin had told him that there was no time to lose. So he concentrated his mind . . . and his shape began to change. His legs seemed to fuse together; shining scales appeared on them as his feet became fins, and suddenly he was no longer human but a merboy with a fishlike tail. Arhans whistled approval and their speed increased as they headed through the forest.

Within minutes they saw a shape moving more slowly ahead of them, and as they drew closer the shape resolved into the figure of a mermaid. She was picking seaweed and putting it in a woven bag that was slung over one shoulder. Her long golden hair flowed around her, and they could hear her singing to herself as she worked.

'Mother!' The boy put on a last burst of speed and rushed up to the mermaid in a swirl of bubbles.

'Kes?' The mermaid, whose name was Morvyr, smiled a welcome, then saw the dolphin. 'And Arhans too. What are you both doing here?'

'Mother, there's trouble!' Kes said breathlessly. 'Arhans came to warn us – she says we're in danger!'

Morvyr's smile changed to a frown. 'Danger? What kind of danger?'

Arhans answered with a stream of whistling and chittering, and as she listened Morvyr's eyes grew wide with alarm, for the dolphin's message was simple and stark. Taran, Queen of the mermaids, was planning to arrest Morvyr.

'*Arrest* me?' Morvyr exclaimed. 'But why? What have I done wrong?'

Arhans did not know, but there was no doubting it, she communicated. She and her friends had heard the news from their cousins. Taran had already sent her henchmen to find Morvyr and take her captive – and it had something to do with a silver pearl.

'The pearl that's hidden in Lizzy's locket!' Kes gasped, horrified. 'The Queen must have found out about it somehow – and that means she must know about Lizzy too. Oh, Mother, what are we going to do?'

'I can guess Taran's plan,' said Morvyr grimly. 'She means to hold me hostage, to make Lizzy give her the silver pearl.'

'But why?' asked Kes. 'What's so special about it? Mother, why won't you explain the mystery?'

'I've told you before: it's far safer if you and Lizzy don't know the whole story, at least not yet.' Morvyr looked around at the flowing fronds of weed. 'Taran's henchmen could come at any time. Whatever else happens, she must *not* get her hands on the pearl! There's only one thing to do, Kes. We'll have to go into hiding.'

Kes was aghast. 'Where?'

'The dolphins will find us a safe place.' Arhans chittered agreement, and Morvyr stroked her smooth head. 'We're so grateful to you, Arhans! Now, we daren't waste a moment. We must set off at once.'

'Mother, what about Lizzy? I promised to meet her today –'

'Then you'll have to break your promise. Neither of us can risk seeing anyone until this is over.'

'But Lizzy'll be frantic with worry! Can't I at least try to reach her through the shell I gave her?'

'No, Kes, it's too dangerous. Until we're safe in hiding, we daren't try to contact her in case Taran's servants overhear. We must leave everything and everyone behind, and go now!'

Kes tried to argue but Morvyr was immovable, and eventually he gave up.

Arhans had sent out a call to her friends, and now five more dolphins arrived. They knew a hiding place that Taran's servants would never find, and they urged Morvyr and Kes to go with them as quickly as possible. Two dolphins went ahead to make sure that the way was safe, and Arhans and the other three flanked Kes and his mother as they swam away through the kelp.

They had not been gone more than a few minutes when, not far away, there was a sudden disturbance in the oar-weed forest and five of Queen Taran's servants emerged in front of Kes and Morvyr's cave. Tullor led them; with the rest crowding behind him he swam to the entrance curtain and thrust his huge ugly head through it. One look was enough. The cave was untidy, and there was half-eaten food on the rock that served as a table. The occupants had obviously left in a hurry.

With a savage hiss Tullor withdrew. 'They

have gone!' he snarled. 'Someone must have warned them – they have escaped!'

Thinking fast, he gave orders. Morvyr and Kes must be found – if they were not, the Queen's fury would have no limit and they would all suffer! Immediately the other creatures set off to start the search; but Tullor called one of them back. It was a huge cuttlefish, and as it hovered in front of him, its long tentacles quivering and its savage beak snapping, he said, 'We too will search for the mermaid and her son. But first we will destroy their home, as a warning to others. We will show them what becomes of anyone who dares to disobey our Queen!'

A shudder of pleasure ran the length of the cuttlefish's body. Then the two of them swam through the seaweed curtain into the cave.

Chapter Two

Though it was still early, the sun was hot
when Lizzy arrived at the beach not far
from the harbour. From a distance she could
hear the cheerful sounds of summer
holidaymakers. The beach was already
crowded; people swam or surfed in the sea,
played games on the sand and fished in the
rock pools, watched attentively by the
lifeguards from their 4x4 truck parked well
clear of the tideline.

Lizzy found herself a spot at one end of
the beach, near the low headland where a
small automatic lighthouse stood. Dumping

her striped drawstring bag on a handy rock, she stripped down to her swimsuit, stuffed her clothes and sandals into the bag then flopped on to the sand. She was early; Kes wouldn't turn up for a little while yet, so she gazed at the sea, watching the swimmers and surfers in the water.

She thought back to the first time she had met Kes. She had lost her locket in the sea and was desperately searching along the beach to see if it had been washed ashore. Miraculously Kes had found it, they had started talking . . . And she had discovered that Kes was her brother, and though their father was human, their mother was a mermaid . . .

She remembered the shock and wonder of it all as clearly as when it had begun. The discovery that she could breathe and speak underwater. The first meeting with Morvyr, her mother. The encounters with Arhans and the other dolphins, and the first steps she had taken towards understanding their

18

strange language. She was so eager to see them all again, to swim with Kes, to see the cave where he and Morvyr lived, to *be* with them.

Impatiently she looked at her watch, and was surprised to see how much time had passed. Kes should have arrived by now, but when she shielded her eyes against the dazzling sunlight she couldn't see him on the beach or in the water. But he was sure to turn up at any moment. She'd better get ready. Reaching for her bag, she took out her wetsuit and wrestled herself into it. A final twist and wriggle as she pulled up the zip at the back of her neck, then she sprinted towards the sea. At the water's edge she stopped, letting the small wavelets curdle around her feet. The wind whisked her short blonde curls round her face; she pushed them back, blinking her blue eyes as she watched the sea. She waited a few minutes, then a few more. But there was still no sign of Kes.

Where was he? He should be here by now. Though there were no such things as clocks in the undersea world, he had always been on time before. Was something wrong?

She waded into the sea until she was waist-deep and the waves were breaking around her. Maybe Kes was playing a joke – she wouldn't put it past him to be waiting under the water not far from shore, ready to dart out and startle her when she least expected it. *All right*, Lizzy thought, grinning to herself. *We'll see about that!*

A bigger wave broke and she let it lift her off her feet, then began to swim further out. One quick glance to make sure the lifeguards weren't looking . . . the next wave rolled towards her, and Lizzy launched herself towards it and dived under the water.

She couldn't see much at first, for the rolling waves were churning up the sand and making everything murky. But, as she reached deeper, calmer water she left the swirling grains behind and the sea became clear, translucent blue-green. Lizzy took a breath, watching bubbles stream from her mouth and up to the surface. A shoal of silvery phosphorescent fish – mackerel, she thought – dashed past in the opposite direction, and patches of drifting seaweed rolled and flowed in the current. Weed would make a good hiding place. But when she plunged in among the strands she found only a small crab and several bright yellow periwinkles hitching a ride.

Lizzy was starting to worry. If Kes couldn't meet her for some reason, surely he would have asked Arhans to come in his place, and though she hadn't learned to understand the dolphins properly yet, she would have got the idea. Something *must* be wrong.

Lizzy didn't know what to do for the best. Probably the most sensible thing would be to go back to the beach and hope that either Kes or Arhans would eventually turn up. But just sitting around and waiting didn't appeal. She wanted to *do* something.

While she tried to make her mind up, the current was carrying her further out to sea. The sandy bed was a long way below her now, and all around she could hear the more powerful sound of the deep ocean. There were fish everywhere, but nothing big enough to be Kes or a dolphin – until in the distance she saw a much larger shape swimming across her path.

Hope sprang up and Lizzy called eagerly, 'Arhans?'

The shape slowed and then turned towards her, but it gave no answering whistle as Arhans would have done. Uncertainly Lizzy watched as it came towards her. Then her eyes widened in alarm as she saw it more clearly.

It was a conger eel – but never in her life

had Lizzy imagined, let alone seen, such a giant. It must have been five metres long from its blunt, ugly snout to the tip of its writhing tail. Its skin was dark grey, almost black, and its cold, fishlike eyes stared at her in a way that was hypnotizing. Lizzy wanted to scream – but what would be the use, when none of her friends were here to help her?

Then to her astonishment the eel's mouth opened, revealing rows of ferocious teeth, and it said in a husky, hissing voice, 'Please don't be afraid of me!'

It could *speak*! Lizzy was so stunned that she forgot her fear. The eel wriggled, sending ripples down the whole length of its body. 'Please,' it repeated, 'I mean no harm, but I must talk to you. Are you the one called . . . Lizzy?'

Lizzy's mouth worked, but for a few moments she couldn't answer. At last she managed, 'Y-yes . . .'

'I am so glad to have found you! I have been looking for you. I am a friend of your father.'

Lizzy's blue eyes opened wide. 'My *father*? But – but he disappeared! No one has heard of him for years!'

'I know this. Now, though, there is news. I heard it from another friend; I did not believe it at first, but there is proof. Your father is alive.'

A choking feeling came into Lizzy's throat. Her real father, Jack Carrick, had been a local fisherman. Lizzy now knew that she had been stolen as a baby and that her father had gone in search of her, leaving Morvyr and Kes behind, and had never returned. Now, suddenly, this creature claimed to have news of him!

'Wh-where is he?' she asked, barely able to get the words out.

The giant eel dipped its head. 'I do not know. But the friend I spoke to claims to

have seen him. I can take you to that friend,
if you wish it.'

Though Lizzy was starting to feel wildly
excited, a scrap of caution warned her to be
careful. How could she be sure that this
creature was telling the truth? There were
enemies in the sea, as well as friends . . .

'If your friend knows about my father,' she
said, 'why didn't he tell us himself? And why
did you come to me? Why didn't you go to
Morvyr?'

The eel made a sound that was almost
like a sigh. 'The merfolk find me hideous.
Whenever they see me, they drive me
away. I know I look hideous to you too.
But I thought . . . I hoped . . . that you
might overlook my ugliness and talk to
me. As for my friend . . . he is even uglier
than I am. So we are both too afraid to go
to Morvyr. Afraid and . . .' His voice
dropped almost to a whisper. '. . .
ashamed.'

Lizzy's kind heart was touched. The eel *was* ugly, certainly. But, as she listened to his sad confession, her fear and revulsion melted. The creature couldn't help his appearance. And if he and his friend had news of her father, and were willing to tell her what they knew, then as far as she was concerned they were her friends too.

The eel had lowered his head again, as if he couldn't find the courage to look her in the eye. Lizzy reached out and, very gently, touched the top of his head.

'Poor eel,' she said sympathetically. 'I understand. Thank you for being brave enough to talk to me.'

The eel's head came up, and though his eyes were fishlike and expressionless she thought he looked hopeful. 'Then – will you come and meet my friend?' he asked.

'Yes, I will!' Lizzy forgot Kes and her worries. The eel's story had convinced her, and all she could think of was this incredible

chance to learn more about her long-lost
father. 'When can we go?'

'Now!' The eel wriggled eagerly. 'Why not?
I will lead, and all you have to do is follow
me!'

He writhed his long body round and set
off. For a moment Lizzy hesitated. Then,
with excitement spinning giddily through her
mind, she swam after him.

Chapter Three

Despite his size the giant eel moved very swiftly, and at first Lizzy thought she was going to be left far behind. But after a minute or so he looked back, saw her and slowed down to wait for her.

'I am sorry,' he said as she caught up. 'I had forgotten that you have lived on land for many years and are not yet used to the sea.'

Lizzy smiled at him. 'I'm learning fast.'

'So I see. Your father will be proud.' He swam on, but more slowly, and Lizzy kept pace beside him. They seemed to be heading out to sea rather than along the coast, and she wondered where he was leading her and how long it would take to get there. She was beginning to feel nervous, for she had never ventured this far out before. The water was colder than she was used to, the current stronger and the sunlight didn't seem to reach so far down, so that the colours around her were strange and dark and just a little menacing. She asked how much further they had to go, but the eel didn't seem to hear. He was forging ahead again, and as he swam he frequently turned his head from side to side, as if he were watching for something.

Lizzy didn't see or hear the intruders approaching. The first she knew of it was when the eel suddenly coiled and turned, swirling the water around him, and uttered a furious hiss.

'What is it?' Lizzy called.

Ignoring her, the eel hissed again. It was a terrifying sound, savage and cruel. His

mouth opened, revealing his ferocious teeth –
then above the sounds he was making Lizzy
heard whistling cries, and five streamlined
shapes appeared out of the murk. Dolphins –
and the leading one had a line of silver along
its back. They streaked towards Lizzy and
the giant eel, and in relief Lizzy cried, 'It's
Arhans! Don't be afraid, eel! Arhans –
Arhans, it's all right! The eel's a friend; he's
got news of my father!'

She hardly had time to finish before a
backwash set her spinning as Arhans hurtled
past and headed straight for the eel. His tail
thrashed; he tried to dart out of the dolphin's
path, but he wasn't quick enough and
Arhans's snout slammed into him, sending
him reeling and twisting backwards.

'Arhans!' Lizzy screamed. 'Stop, oh, stop
it! He's my *friend*!'

Arhans took no notice, and now the other
dolphins joined the attack. They were all
whistling shrilly. The eel snarled, his teeth

snapping at them, and for some moments Lizzy could see nothing but churning water and flailing fins and tails. Then suddenly the eel broke free from the struggling group. He looked, once, in Lizzy's direction, and his hideous face seemed to twist with fury and hatred before, with a flick of his powerful tail, he swam away at top speed. Two of the dolphins surged in pursuit, while the other three, with Arhans in the lead, came to Lizzy. Arhans was chittering urgently; the sounds she made seemed to form a word in Lizzy's mind. *Tullor, Tullor* . . . It was something to do with the eel, Lizzy was sure. His name, maybe? If only she had learned more of the dolphins' language!

'He was trying to help me!' she protested. 'He was taking me to meet someone who knows where my father is!'

There was anger in Arhans's answering whistle, and Lizzy felt as if she were saying, *No, no, that's wrong!* The other dolphins nosed Lizzy anxiously as though making sure she wasn't injured, and Arhans rubbed her face gently against Lizzy's cheek. Though she couldn't understand most of Arhans's words, Lizzy began to realize what she meant. The eel wasn't a friend at all, but had been trying to deceive her. *Danger!* Arhans seemed to be telling her. *Great danger!*

'Danger to me?' Lizzy was alarmed. 'But why should that eel want to hurt me? Oh, if only Kes was here! Why didn't he meet me like he promised?'

All three dolphins answered with a chorus of agitated noises. *Danger* again – but this time they weren't talking about Lizzy. Kes and Morvyr were in danger too!

'What kind of danger?' Lizzy cried. 'Where are they?'

Again she didn't know exactly what Arhans replied, but she understood enough to get an idea of what had happened. Morvyr was afraid of something; she had gone into hiding and taken Kes with her. Whatever happened, Lizzy must *not* try to find them. As she communicated this warning Arhans started to nudge at Lizzy, gently but very firmly. The others joined in, and she realized that they were trying to urge her back to the shore. They were saying it was dangerous for her to stay here. They were saying it was dangerous to visit the undersea world at all.

There were three of them, they were much stronger than she was and they were determined to make her do what they wanted. Though she desperately wanted to start searching for Kes and Morvyr, Lizzy had no choice, and went with them. They surfaced near the lighthouse, out of sight of the beach. Lizzy climbed on to the rocks – it was an easy scramble from here to the top – and looked back at the three dolphins in the water.

'I'll be on the beach every morning,' she said. 'If there's any news, anything at all, come and find me. Please, Arhans! Please!'

Arhans gave a clear, piercing whistle. Then, swiftly and smoothly, the dolphins dived under the water and were gone.

There was no one in the house when Lizzy got home. Mr Baxter was being shown round the college where he was to teach after the summer holidays. Mrs Baxter was a part-time administrator at the hospital in Truro, and this was one of her work days, and Rose was probably out with Paul.

Lizzy ran upstairs to her bedroom. On a shelf among her ornaments was a large, tapering spiral shell. Kes had given it to her the first time she had ventured under the sea, and he had told her that she could use it to communicate with him or with the dolphins when she was on land. 'All you have to do is hold the shell to your ear, and we'll be with you,' he had said. Eagerly Lizzy snatched up the shell and put it to her ear. But though she could hear the hissing, roaring sounds of the sea, there was nothing else. No distant voice, no sense that anyone was there at all. Wherever Kes had gone, he either could not or dared not call to her. And she, in her turn, didn't dare try to call to him.

She put the shell back on its shelf and went downstairs again, her feet dragging and her shoulders slumped. The house suddenly felt empty and lonely, and she would have given anything to have someone to talk to. But then she thought: if anyone had been here, what could she have said? Even Rose didn't know her secret; she thought Kes was just an ordinary local boy. There was no one she could tell. No one she could share her worry with. All she could do was wait.

Chapter Four

Tullor was tired, angry – and frightened. The two dolphins had chased him for more than an hour, and by the time he finally managed to give them the slip and get away, he was exhausted. He had always hated the dolphins, but now that they had foiled his plan to lure and capture the girl-child, he hated them more than ever. And when Queen Taran found out what had happened, her fury would be terrible.

He would have to tell her soon, and he dreaded it. But the longer he waited, the greater her rage would be. It would be better

to gather his courage, go to her now and get
it over with.

Cautiously he poked his head out from
under the rock ledge where he had been
hiding. The dolphins had lost sight of
him when he'd wriggled under here and he
felt sure they must have swum away by
now. But it was wiser to be careful, so he
peered through the underwater gloom in
case they might still be lurking nearby.
There was no sign of them, and, relieved,
Tullor wriggled out from his hole and tried
to work out where he was. The chase had
taken him many miles out to sea, and the
gateway by which he usually reached
Queen Taran's cave was a long, long way
off. But there were other gateways, and
his instinct told him that one of them was
nearby.

He soon found it: a great, solitary rock on
the seabed, with a deep hollow gouged in the
top. Tullor swam to it, hovered above the

hollow and waited. A minute passed, then a voice whispered coldly out of the hollow, '*Who is there?*'

Summoning all his nerve, Tullor replied, 'It is Tullor.'

'*Ah!*' The voice was full of satisfaction. '*You may enter!*'

The water started to swirl and bubble, then the hollow became a tunnel with an eerie green light glowing from deep inside it. The light shone on Tullor's face, and a shiver of fear ran through him. But it was too late to turn back now.

He gave a writhing squirm, and dived into the hole. For a second or two he saw only the green light, then it changed, becoming all the colours of the rainbow, and moments later he surfaced in the perfectly circular pool inside the mermaid Queen's lair.

Taran was lying on her rock couch. Her eyes were brilliant with excitement and there was a triumphant smile on her face. But when she saw that Tullor was alone, her expression changed.

'Where is the girl-child?' she hissed.

'Majesty, I – I found her, and I spoke to her as you commanded, but –'

'But what?' Taran snapped. 'What went wrong? Were you stupid enough to give the truth away?'

'No, Majesty!' Tullor protested. 'She believed my story! She was coming with me! But the dolphins saw us, and they attacked – there were five of them, and I had no time to call for help!'

'You mean the child escaped?' Taran's voice rose shrilly. 'You fool! You stupid, useless, worthless *fool*!'

'There was nothing I could do!' cried Tullor desperately. 'Three of the dolphins took the girl to safety, and the other two chased me. I barely escaped with my life!'

Taran let out a shriek of rage that echoed around the cave. 'They should have killed you!' she screamed. 'It's no more than you deserve!' She raised a hand high above her head, as though about to throw something, and Tullor cried, 'No, Majesty, please – I did my best! Truly, I did my best!'

Taran was too furious to listen. Her hand came down with a violent gesture and the water around Tullor erupted into a seething, churning whirlpool. The huge eel was flung about, thrashing and struggling as the water battered him against the pool's rock edges. He howled in terror, then with a tremendous effort he dived deep, deep down into the water, desperate to escape.

Taran saw him vanish. She made another gesture and the water calmed. In moments it was as still and quiet as a mirror again. The Queen stared down into it. She knew that Tullor was cowering at the bottom of the pool, and her beautiful face turned ugly with anger.

'I know where you are!' she snarled. 'And

you can stay there until I give you permission to return – *if* I ever do!'

There was no answer, but Taran was certain that the eel had heard her. Suddenly she reached to a rock shelf behind her couch and snatched up her golden circlet with the seven pearls set in it. The circlet was more than just her crown: it gave her *power*. She set it carefully on her head and felt the power begin to flow through her. She wouldn't punish Tullor any more. He was too useful and, besides, the dolphins were really the ones to blame for his failure. Very well, then. She would vent her fury on them, and on all the wretched creatures who had helped Morvyr and her children to escape. She would show them the price of defying their Queen, in a way they wouldn't forget for a long time!

Taran spread her arms wide, drew a deep breath and closed her eyes. *Darkness. Rage. Peril . . .*

The water in the pool churned again, and a wind sprang up from nowhere and began to moan through the cave . . .

Rose had brought Paul home for tea, and they were all in the middle of the meal when Mr Baxter peered out of the sitting-room window and said, 'Whew, I don't like the look of that sky!'

Mrs Baxter and Rose got up from the table and went to see too. 'Wow!' said Rose. 'Your dad was right, Paul. There *is* going to be a storm!'

'And soon, I should think,' Mrs Baxter added. 'Whoever would have thought it, after such a sunny day.'

'I think Dad must smell them coming,' said Paul with a grin. 'I'd never have guessed, either, and there was nothing on the forecast.'

Rose sat down again. 'Well, I'm glad he did smell it. If you'd gone to sea like you were going to . . .' She shuddered. 'Scary!'

'Yeah.' Paul ate another mouthful of lasagne. 'Though quite a few of the boats are out.' He frowned. 'I hope they make it back to the harbour before this really blows up.'

Lizzy, too, was staring at the window, but she said nothing. Kes had never told her what happened in the undersea world during a storm, so she could only imagine what it was like. The thought frightened her. Would Kes and Morvyr be all right? And what about the dolphins?

'Lizzy, you've hardly eaten anything,' said Mum. 'Are you feeling OK?'

'What? Oh – yes, I'm fine. Just not very hungry.'

Dad smiled kindly. 'Don't worry, love; a storm doesn't always mean thunder. Even if it does, you're much less scared of thunder and lightning than you used to be, aren't you?'

Lizzy couldn't tell him that it wasn't thunder and lightning that worried her, so she just nodded.

'You ought to go home before the rain starts, Paul,' said Mum. 'Or you'll get soaked.'

'Don't be daft, Mum,' said Rose. 'He's a fisherman. He's used to it!'

The chatter went on, but Lizzy wasn't really listening. She made herself eat a few more mouthfuls, but the lasagne could have been made from cardboard and chalk for all she cared. *Where are Kes and Morvyr? Will they be safe tonight?*

The wind was howling now. Some scraps of litter went flying madly down the street, and in the distance there was a rattle that sounded like a dustbin being blown over. As well as the wind Lizzy could hear the sea grumbling ominously. Then a first flurry of rain spattered against the window pane, and moments later the heavens opened.

Paul said he should go, because he had to help his dad make sure their boat was securely moored. He was saying goodbye and thanks for the food, and Rose was arguing with Mum because she wanted to go to the harbour too and Mum said she wasn't going anywhere in this weather and besides she'd only get in the way. Lizzy took no notice but stared out at the worsening storm. She had never seen such a downpour. Water streamed down the window in rivers, and the battering rain was bouncing off the road. The sky was the colour of a bruise, and though it wasn't evening yet, it was getting darker and darker outside.

Rose finally gave up arguing with Mum, and saw Paul off. Wind and rain came whirling into the house when she opened the front door, and as Paul hurried away down the hill with his jacket over his head she had to struggle to get the door shut again.

'Ugh!' she said as she came back to the

sitting room. 'Maybe I don't want to go to the harbour after all.'

'Your face and hair are wet already,' Mum commented.

'I know. This has come on so quickly, hasn't it? It's really weird.'

'I was thinking that,' said Dad. 'I mean, I know we're on the coast and the weather can change very fast, but it's strange that the forecast didn't even mention it. And it was glorious till a couple of hours ago. It doesn't seem natural.'

Lizzy shivered inwardly at that. She, too, thought there was something wrong. The storm had blown up *so* suddenly and *so* violently, as if some unknown force had deliberately caused it to happen. Kes had told her that Taran, the mermaid Queen, was very powerful. Could she be behind this? Could she conjure storms? And, if she could, why had she done it?

Mum and Dad were clearing the table,

while Rose had switched the TV on and was looking for the local news. Suddenly Lizzy wanted to escape to her room. She felt sick with tension and worry. If she stayed here with the rest of the family, someone would be sure to notice.

'Can't find any news,' said Rose, 'but there's a really good movie on in a minute.'

'Sounds fine to me,' said Dad as he carried out a pile of plates. 'In this weather, I can't think of anything better.'

'I . . . um . . . think I'll go upstairs,' Lizzy murmured. 'I've got a few things to do on my computer.'

The computer was always a good excuse. The others would think she was going to spend the evening playing games on it, and they wouldn't ask any awkward questions. Rose said, 'Boring! I'm going to watch the movie,' but Lizzy didn't answer. At the door she paused, looking back into the room. It all looked so *normal* . . .

'See you later,' she said.

'Sure.' Rose wasn't concentrating; she had plonked down on the sofa and was looking at the TV screen. Lizzy hesitated a moment longer, then hurried up the stairs.

Chapter Five

The storm worsened as the evening went
on. There was no lightning or thunder,
but the rain was torrential and a full gale
was blowing. Though Lizzy tried her best
to ignore it, it was impossible. Even when
she played loud music through her
headphones she couldn't completely shut
out the howl of the wind and the noise of
the sea, which wasn't merely grumbling now
but roaring like a hundred angry lions. The
lights kept dimming too, and every time it
happened it made her jump.

Rose went to bed early, and Mum and

Dad weren't far behind her. By half past ten the house was in darkness. Lizzy snuggled under her duvet, shutting her eyes and trying to make herself sleep. But she couldn't. All she could think about was Kes and Morvyr.

She did doze off eventually; at least she must have done, because when the deafening *BANG* came she jolted awake and shot upright in bed with a cry of fright. *Whatever –?*

A second explosion made her scream again. It was a thunderbolt – it must have been! Then her door opened and Mum came in, switching the light on.

'Lizzy, are you all right?'

Lizzy turned to her, white-faced and terrified. 'Oh, Mum! Have we been hit by lightning?'

'No, love! The lifeboat's been called out. That noise was the maroon rockets – they fire them from the station and they probably exploded right above us.' Mum went to the window and lifted back the curtain. 'There are lights going on in lots of houses. What an awful night for a rescue!'

Lizzy was hugely relieved that it hadn't been a thunderbolt, but her relief was quickly swamped by another fear: for the lifeboat crew, and for whoever was in danger out there on the sea.

She scrambled out of bed and joined Mum at the window. Through the streaming glass they glimpsed two dark figures in waterproofs running past the house. This street was halfway up the cliffside hill; lights were coming on in the rows of houses below them, and over the rooftops Lizzy could see more lights blazing in the lifeboat station building. From the headland the beam of the lighthouse swung slowly in from the sea and over the scene. It made everything look unreal and nightmarish.

Rose ran in then and crowded to the window too, elbowing Lizzy aside. 'Is it a shout?' she asked worriedly.

'What?' Lizzy was perplexed.

'A shout – it's what they call it when the lifeboat goes out. Paul told me. His dad's in the crew. Oh, I hope he'll be OK!'

Another man raced past the window, and the headlights of a car rushed along the harbourside road. 'I want to ring Paul!' Rose said.

'No, love, leave him,' Mum told her. 'He's got enough to worry about; he won't be able to talk to you now.'

'But –' Then Rose saw sense. 'If anything awful happens . . .' she finished in a small, scared voice.

'They know what they're doing,' Mum soothed. 'They'll be all right. Don't worry. Look, I don't suppose anyone wants to go back to sleep, so why don't I go downstairs and make us all some tea? Then we can listen to the local radio station, and we'll hear if there's any news.'

She went out, but Rose and Lizzy stayed at the window. Neither of them said anything, but Rose put an arm round Lizzy's shoulders. She seemed to be trying to comfort herself.

The girls tried to locate the lifeboat at the end of its floating pontoon. They couldn't make it out, and certainly didn't hear the engines starting over the noise of the wind and rain, but they saw a dim glow inside the cockpit, and the brighter white stern light. Moments later the lights began to move steadily as the boat set out for sea.

'There they go.' Rose didn't sound like herself. 'I wish there was something we could do to help.'

Lizzy nodded. 'Me too.' She glanced at her sister. 'Do you think Paul's dad's on board?'

'I don't know. Paul says it's up to the captain – I mean, the coxswain. He picks the crew from whoever shows up. I sort of . . .

hope Mr Treleaven didn't get there in time.'

From downstairs came the mumble of the radio, and Mr Baxter, wearing jeans and a sweatshirt, put his head round the door.

'You girls all right?' he asked.

'We're fine, Dad,' Lizzy told him. 'The lifeboat's just gone. We saw it.'

'Well, let's wish them good luck. Coming for a cup of tea?'

Rose was still staring out of the window, though the lifeboat's lights had faded into the murky darkness. 'Come on,' Lizzy said to her. 'There's nothing else to see now.'

Rose hesitated, then nodded and followed her downstairs.

The Baxters drank their tea, then they all went back to bed. Lizzy managed to sleep for a while, but woke as it was starting to get light. It was half past five. The rain had stopped, though the wind still blew gustily. After the uproar of the storm the world

seemed astonishingly quiet. Then she heard
the sound of a diesel engine approaching.

She scrambled out of bed and reached the
window in time to see an ambulance drive
along the harbour road. It was heading for
the lifeboat station – Lizzy's heart skipped,
and she ran across to Rose's room. Rose was
awake, and when Lizzy told her about the
ambulance, her eyes widened with alarm.

'Quick, let's go back – I want to look out
from your window!'

The two girls hurried to Lizzy's room, and
Rose flung the window open, letting in a
whirling gust of wind. Leaning precariously
out, she peered towards the lifeboat
station.

'I can't see where the ambulance went . . .
Oh! Lizzy, the lifeboat's back! I can just
make out the orange top and that radar
thing!'

Lizzy squeezed in to look too, and saw a
bright splash of colour amid the dull greys of

the morning. 'Whoo!' she said. 'What a relief – bet you're glad!'

'You bet I am – but what about the ambulance? Someone must be hurt! What if –'

'It's probably the people they rescued. Rose, be careful – you'll fall out of the window!'

There were noises on the landing, and Mum and Dad appeared, looking sleepy-eyed.

'They're back, they're safe!' Rose told them. 'But an ambulance just went past – Mum, I want to go to the lifeboat station and see what's happened!' She saw Mum hesitate and added, '*Please* – it's light now, and the rain's stopped!'

'We-ell . . .'

'Tell you what,' said Dad. 'Give it half an hour – time for the ambulance crew to do what they have to – and then you can go. But you *mustn't* get in anyone's way, all right?'

'Of course I won't! I'll get dressed.'
Rose ran out of the room. Dad called, '*Not
now, Rose! In half an hour!*' but she didn't
answer.

Rose was jumping with impatience by the
time half an hour had passed and she could
leave for the lifeboat station. Lizzy went with
her. Mum and Dad had been reluctant to let
her, but Rose chimed in on Lizzy's side and
at last they gave way.

'I'm glad you came,' Rose said as they
hurried along the street, heads down against
the wind. 'If Paul's not there, I don't know
anyone else, and if I have to just stand there
out of the way with no one to talk to, I
think I'll explode!'

There was a small crowd around the
lifeboat station. The ambulance had gone,
but the coastguards were there, and a police
car, and the harbour master and several
fishermen. The lifeboat itself was back at its
mooring, tilting and swaying with the swell,

and beyond the harbour the sea was a mass of tumbling white horses.

Rose saw Paul standing by the wall of the station building, and ran to him. 'Paul! Did your dad go out? Is he all right?'

Paul smiled broadly. 'He's fine. Some of them were a bit seasick, though.'

'What happened? We saw the ambulance from Lizzy's window.'

'It was for the guys they rescued. They're the crew of a French fishing trawler; they lost their rudder, then started taking on water. The trawler sank, but the lifeboat got everyone off.'

Rose let out her breath in a huge, huffing sigh. 'It must have been really hairy! So who got hurt?'

'They've taken all the crew to hospital, of course, just to check them out. But apparently one guy fell overboard. They got him out of the water but he's unconscious and they don't know how bad he is yet.'

Paul frowned. 'There was something a bit weird about it . . .'

Lizzy felt a sudden inward shiver that she couldn't explain. 'What do you mean, weird?' she asked.

'Nobody on the lifeboat can speak much French, so they weren't exactly sure what the trawlermen said, but it looks as if no one really knows anything about this guy.'

'What, he was a new crew member, you mean?' asked Rose.

'I suppose so. But Dad said they didn't even know his name. And that's not the only thing. When he went overboard, no one saw it happen. But, when the lifeboat got a line to the trawler, a whole lot of dolphins suddenly appeared and started jumping around, like they were trying to attract attention. They were making a huge fuss, so the cox turned the searchlight on them, and there in the middle of them was this French guy!'

Lizzy and Rose both stared at him in astonishment, then Lizzy whispered, 'The dolphins were helping him?'

'Looks like it. They found him and held him up till he was rescued.'

'Wow!' said Rose, awed. 'I've heard stories about dolphins doing things like that, but . . . Wow!' She looked at Lizzy. 'Isn't that *amazing*?'

Lizzy was staring at the lifeboat. She wanted to ask, how many dolphins were there? Did one have a silver streak on its back? Above all, did they know, somehow, who the mysterious Frenchman was? But, if she asked, there would be too much to explain. So she just said:

'Yes. Amazing . . .'

Chapter Six

By mid-morning the town was buzzing with the story of the rescue. Everyone seemed to have heard about the dolphins, and there were all kinds of rumours about who the man they had saved might be. Lizzy went to the beach, hoping that Arhans might appear, but there was no sign, and the lifeguards warned her not to go in the sea because of the rough waves and dangerous swell.

Mum had been working at the hospital again, and when she came home late that afternoon she had more news of the French crew.

'The man who was pulled out of the sea's going to be all right,' she told them. 'But he really *is* a mystery man. Apparently the skipper said he isn't one of their regular crew and all he knows about him is his name. But that's odd too, because his name's Kernewek which just means "Cornish" in the old Cornish language.'

'Sounds as if he didn't want them to know his real identity,' said Dad.

Rose grinned. 'Maybe he's committed a huge fraud or something, and he's on the run from the French police.'

'Maybe, though he doesn't look the type,' said Mum.

'Oh, well, I expect our police may want to talk to him,' said Dad. 'Has he regained consciousness yet?'

'Yes, but he's not making much sense I was talking to the ward sister earlier, and she told me that he just keeps repeating the same thing over and over again. It's a funny word;

now, what was it . . .?' Mum frowned, thinking. 'Oh, yes: "Tegenn". Something like that, anyway.'

Dad shook his head. 'Never heard anything like it before.'

'Nor me,' Rose added.

No one was looking at Lizzy. But she felt as if her insides had suddenly frozen up and locked solid. *Tegenn* . . .

It was the name that her real parents had given her when she was born under the sea.

By the following morning Lizzy was so pent-up that she thought she might snap in half. She was desperate to find out more about the stranger in the hospital, but she couldn't question Mum without making her suspicious. Besides, Mum had already told the family what little she knew and, to make matters worse, she wasn't working today. Short of going to the hospital herself – which was out of the question, of course – there was nothing Lizzy could do.

She spent the day roaming the beach and the coast path, hoping that she would see the dolphins. She ached to tell Arhans what was happening, and to ask her what had happened on the night of the rescue. She was frantic, too, for any news of Kes and Morvyr. But none of the dolphins appeared. And, even if they had, Lizzy reminded herself miserably, she hadn't learned their speech yet and wouldn't understand much of what they told her. Though the thought was almost more than she could bear, she would just have to wait until Mum went back to work and brought home more news.

But, when news did come, it wasn't Mum who brought it. Rose had been out with Paul all afternoon, and arrived home just after tea. It was Lizzy's turn to wash the dishes; Dad was drying for her and they both looked up as Rose came into the kitchen.

'Hi, slaves,' said Rose cheerfully.

'Cheek!' Dad flipped the tea towel at her. 'Have a nice afternoon?'

'Yeah, cool. Oh, by the way, something really random, you know that guy –'

Mum came in from the garden at that moment. 'What guy?' she asked curiously. 'What's all this?'

Dad grinned. 'We were just about to find out. Sounds to me like Rose has got herself two boyfriends, instead of just one!'

'Oh, shut up, Dad!' Rose snorted. 'I've been round at Paul's, and something really cool's happened. The guy from the trawler, who's in hospital – he isn't French, he's from round here, and Paul's dad *knows* him!'

Lizzy froze with the soapy sponge in one hand and a plate in the other. Her face was a study in shock, but Rose didn't notice.

'Apparently he was much better this morning, and said he lived here years ago, so they asked him if there were people who'd remember him, and he gave them some names, and one of them was Jeff Treleaven. They used to be best mates! So the hospital rang Paul's dad, and he went in and saw the guy, and it *is* his old mate! What are the chances of *that*?'

Mum said, 'Pretty small, I should think,' and Dad added, 'What a coincidence!'

'Yeah – and he got rescued by the lifeboat from his old home town,' Rose added. 'I mean, talk about *weird*?'

Still Lizzy stared and said nothing.

Rose had more to tell. 'Anyway, they're letting him out of hospital tomorrow. The police and coastguards'll want to talk to him, but it's just routine stuff; he hasn't committed a crime or anything. He's got nowhere to go so he's going to stay at Paul's place till he gets sorted.'

Dad whistled. 'Well, what an extraordinary turn-up!' he said. 'So, what's this long-lost friend's name?'

'He's called Jack,' said Rose. 'Jack Carrick.'

The crash made them all jump, and they stared at the shattered plate, which lay on the floor surrounded by a starburst of soap suds.

'Lizzy!' Mum scolded.

'S-sorry, Mum . . .' Lizzy's face had turned pale. 'It just – slipped.'

'Well, do try to be more careful, love. You'd better get a dry cloth and wipe the floor, while I pick up the pieces.'

Because everyone was distracted by the accident, Lizzy managed to hide her shock from the rest of the family. In fact, though, she was shaking like a jelly. She had hardly dared believe it, but it had to be true. The shipwrecked man must be her real father – and from tomorrow he would be staying at the Treleavens' house! She had to see him. She had to talk to him. She just *had* to!

Mum was asking Rose more about Jack

Carrick, but Lizzy couldn't take in what they were saying. Her mind was spinning with thoughts, plans, ideas, hopes – somehow she finished the washing up without breaking anything else and, as soon as she could, she escaped to her room. There, she grabbed her shell and pressed it to her ear. All she could hear was the familiar, sea-like whooshing. There was no sense of Kes's or the dolphins' presence, and after a minute or so she gave up trying, put the shell back and went to the window, where she sat and looked out over the rooftops. The storm clouds had cleared away and the sun was shining again, but the sea still looked restless and dangerous. There were choppy white wave crests in the bay beyond the harbour; if the dolphins were there, it would be impossible to pick them out from this distance. She could go to the beach again, but what was the point? She'd spent half the day searching for Arhans, but Arhans simply wasn't there. All she could do was try again tomorrow, and until then she would just have to be patient.

That, though, was going to be the hardest thing in the world.

Chapter Seven

The next day was awful for Lizzy.
Though she spent almost all of it at the beach or on the lighthouse headland, there was still no sign of the dolphins. She was desperate to get a message to Kes and Morvyr about Jack Carrick, and Arhans and the others were her only hope. Why didn't they come? Where were they? In spite of Arhans's warning that she should stay away from the sea, Lizzy was tempted to go and search for them. But a red flag was flying on the beach, and to her dismay the lifeguards told her that it meant 'No Bathing'.

'There's still a big swell after the storm, and some treacherous rip currents,' the head lifeguard said.

'Rip currents?' Lizzy echoed.

'Yes. You can't see them, but, if you get caught in one, you can be swept away in moments.' He grinned in a friendly way. 'So, no swimming today, OK? If you went in, we'd have to come after you and heave you out!'

The lifeguards were patrolling the water's edge, so there was no way she could avoid being seen if she tried to disobey the flag warning. She could go to the lighthouse, of course, then climb down the rocks of the headland and reach the sea from there. But, if she found herself caught in a rip current, was she a strong enough swimmer to get out of trouble? Though it was a bitter disappointment, she dared not take the risk.

By evening Lizzy felt as if her insides were

boiling with frustration, and Rose only made matters worse. She had been out with Paul again, and when she got home she said that Jack Carrick had arrived at the Treleavens'.

'I'll probably meet him tomorrow night,' she added casually. 'I'm going round to Paul's, and I expect he'll be there.'

Lizzy's heart started to thump. 'Can I come with you?' she asked hopefully.

'No, you can't. Don't be so silly! Why on earth would he want you tagging along to gawp at him? You're a complete stranger.'

The words *a complete stranger* really stung Lizzy. But of course Rose didn't know the real story, and Lizzy couldn't tell her.

Tomorrow, she told herself, she *would* find Arhans, and even the lifeguards wouldn't stop her. But in the morning Mum said that she was taking both the girls to Truro to get uniforms for their new school.

Rose groaned, and Lizzy's face fell. 'Oh, Mum! School doesn't start for another month – I can't think about it now! I wanted to go to the beach.'

'You've spent just about all your time at the beach since we moved in,' Mum said firmly. 'One day away from it won't hurt. We're going, and that's that.'

'Cheer up,' said Rose, seeing Lizzy's expression. 'At least if we get this over and done with now, we can forget about school again till September.'

Lizzy didn't answer. They drove to Truro, and somehow she got through the dreary business of trying on blazers and skirts and sports kit. Even a delicious and expensive lunch didn't help. And by the time they got home, after crawling through heavy traffic, the day was almost over and she couldn't find an excuse to get away and look for the dolphins.

Rose went out in the evening, and didn't come in until after Lizzy had gone to bed. Next morning, though, she had news.

'I met Mr Carrick,' she told the family over breakfast. 'He's really nice – you'd like him, Dad – he's got a ghastly sense of humour just like yours.'

'Cheek!' said Dad, grinning.

'Has he settled in all right?' Mum asked.

'Oh, yes. I mean, the police have talked to him, of course, and Social Services have been round, and the local press are trying to get hold of him and all that, but he's cool about it.' Rose helped herself to cereal. 'Know what he told Paul? He just wants to get out on his own in a boat, and have a bit of peace and quiet.'

'Oh, he's a sailing man, is he?' Dad looked interested; learning to sail was one of the things he planned to do.

'Mmm,' Rose said with her mouth full, then swallowed. 'Paul's dad's got a boat – a small one, I mean, as well as his trawler.' She laughed. 'He reckons there'll be hordes of reporters calling round today; he's lending

Mr Carrick the boat so he can get away before they turn up!'

Mum smiled. 'Good for him! I should think a grilling from the press is the last thing he wants.'

'*I* wouldn't hide from them,' said Rose. 'I'd make out it was a really massive drama, sell the story to the Sunday papers and make loads of money. Brilliant! Wouldn't you, Lizzy?' She waited. 'Lizzy?'

'What? Oh – sorry, I was miles away.'

'I said, wouldn't you want to talk to the press if you were Jack Carrick?'

'Er . . . I don't know. Maybe.' Lizzy hesitated, then, hoping she sounded casual, asked, 'Where does Paul's dad keep his boat?'

'Somewhere in that marina on the other side of the harbour, I think.'

'Oh, right. What's it called?'

'You mean, what's *she* called,' Rose corrected. 'You always say *she* when you talk about boats.'

'Well, she, then.'

'Dunno. Silver something; can't remember. Why?'

'I . . . just wondered.'

Rose gave her a strange look, but let it drop. Lizzy, though, was churning with inner excitement. If she could get to the marina before Jack Carrick left . . .

'I don't want any more to eat, Mum,' she said. 'Is it OK if I go out?'

Mum blinked, surprised by the sudden change of subject. 'Yes, I suppose so,' she said. 'Once you've helped clear away and tidied your room. Whose turn is it to wash up?'

'Mine.' Rose pulled a face. 'And you and Dad have had eggs. I *hate* washing egg things. Why can't we get a dishwasher?'

'Because the kitchen's too small for one,' Dad told her. 'Anyway, you keep telling us you're so eco-friendly. What's eco-friendly about dishwashers?'

'Plenty,' said Rose, 'when I've got to wash egg things!'

Lizzy left them cheerfully arguing. She rushed through her chores as fast as she could, then shoved her wetsuit into her bag and set off for the harbour. A boat called *Silver* something . . . it shouldn't be too difficult to find. She just hoped she wouldn't get there too late.

About thirty small boats were tied up in the marina, some with their owners on board preparing for a day's sailing now that the sea was calmer. Lizzy walked along the floating wooden pontoons, trying to get used to their slight swaying as she looked at each boat in turn. She saw *White Gull*, *Red Witch* and *Sungold*, but none of them had a name with *Silver* in it. Thinking that perhaps she had missed it, she was about to start on a second circuit when someone called out to her and she saw Paul approaching.

'Hi, Lizzy.' Paul had a coil of heavy rope slung over his shoulder. 'What are you doing down here?'

'I . . . er . . .' Then Lizzy thought, *Rose isn't here, and Paul won't ask awkward questions* . . . 'I was going to have a look at your dad's sailing boat,' she said.

'What, *Silvie*, you mean? She's not here this morning. Our new guest's taken her out.'

So she *was* too late. 'Oh,' Lizzy said, crestfallen. 'Rose said something about that.'

'Go on, own up!' Paul laughed, but it was a kind laugh. 'It was him you wanted to look at, wasn't it? Rose told me you were interested.'

She felt her face turning red. 'Well . . .'

'You and half the town! Don't worry about it – I expect he'd like to meet you too. You'll have to come round and say hello sometime. Not today, though.' He looked out to sea, then pointed. 'There he is, see? The boat with the dark-red sail, heading down the coast. He wanted to go out on his own, to have a look at some of his old haunts. He and Dad used to go to the caves along there years ago, to watch the seals.'

'Oh. Right.' Lizzy tried to make herself stop shaking. Jack Carrick would be passing the cave where she had first met her real mother. Was it special to him? she wondered. Was he going to search for Morvyr?

Paul's voice brought her back to earth. 'I'd better go – promised I'd help Dad do some work on the trawler. Tell Rose I'll see her later, OK?'

'Yes,' said Lizzy. 'Sure.'

'Bye, then.' Paul hoisted the coil of rope again and walked away. Lizzy stood watching as *Silvie* moved slowly across the bright sea, past the headland and out of sight. Her heart was hammering under her ribs, and she was overwhelmed by a desperate yearning to follow him. But could she do it? Did she have the courage?

She knew the answer. Daunting or not, for her there was no other choice.

Chapter Eight

It only took Lizzy a minute to put on her wetsuit, then she left her bag by the lifeboat station and returned to the pontoons. No one noticed her as she slipped into the sea and dived beneath the surface with hardly a splash. As always, she held her breath for the first few moments underwater, still hardly able to believe in what she could do. Then confidence came back and she opened her mouth, seeing the familiar stream of silver bubbles rush past her face.

When she swam out of the harbour and into the bay, the strength of the current surprised her. It took much more effort than usual to make headway against it. No wonder the lifeguards on the beach were being so careful. The storm tides had churned up the seabed too, and her surroundings were murky. But she could see well enough – just – and she forged towards the headland and the deeper water beyond.

The tide was going out, and once she was clear of the headland swimming became easier. Now the current was working with her rather than against her, and she was able to relax a little. But the undersea world looked very eerie. Even out in the bay the water wasn't its usual clear blue-green. Instead it was full of swirling sand particles, like a weird shifting fog. Mysterious shapes loomed strangely, and tricky shadows lurked in the gloom. Once, Lizzy recoiled in fright when she thought she saw a giant eel writhing towards her, but it was only a long strand of oar-weed drifting in the current.

She surfaced after a while to get her
bearings. She had already come quite a long
way. St Michael's Mount looked smaller than
before, and beyond it she could see the
golden crescent of the beach that curved
along the bay's edge. Treading water, she
turned and looked out to sea. Several small
boats were out there, but they all had white
sails. Where was *Silvie*? She had disappeared!
Anxiously Lizzy turned further, until she
could see the high cliffs stretching away
down the coast to the south-west. They were
dark and forbidding even in the sunlight, and
darker still were the caves, gaping like ragged
black mouths. Which was the cave where she
had met Morvyr? Lizzy couldn't even begin
to guess.

Suddenly she felt frightened. She was alone
in the sea, without Kes or the dolphins to
guide her, searching for a boat that she might
or might not find. It was a crazy, hopeless
thing to do. She should turn back, go home

and find another safer way to make contact with Jack Carrick.

A wave slapped against her face and for a moment everything blurred. Lizzy blinked the water from her eyes – and as her vision cleared she saw something moving against the darkness of the cliffs. A red sail . . . her heart jumped and a tingle went through her from her head to her toes. *Silvie* – it must be! She was sailing slowly, keeping close to the coast, as though whoever was on board were looking for something.

Lizzy's courage came surging back. Surely she could catch up? She had to try, she just *had* to! Kicking out with her legs, she turned until she was directly facing the distant boat, then dived and started to swim towards it with all the energy she could muster.

It wasn't long before she began to tire, and she knew she couldn't keep this pace up for much longer. At last she swam to the surface again, to check how far she had come. She hoped she might see *Silvie* just a short way ahead, but to her dismay she saw that, far from catching up, she was being left behind. A wind had freshened, filling the red sail, and *Silvie* was moving faster, drawing away from her at a speed she couldn't hope to match.

Gasping with exertion and nearly in tears, Lizzy dived again and forged on. If only she could swim faster! Kes could change from human to merboy – she had seen him do it, willing his legs to merge together and become a shining tail. He said that she had the power too, but she had never learned to use it, and it was locked away out of reach in the depths of her mind. Now she tried again with all her strength to unlock it, telling herself desperately that she *was* a mermaid, she *was* a mermaid. But she couldn't turn the key. She just couldn't make it happen!

Then through the water she heard a

strange sound; a deep, rhythmic throbbing that came from further out to sea. The current began to swirl, and in alarm Lizzy headed for the surface again. As her head emerged into the sunlight she saw the cause of the disturbance. A big boat was coming up behind her; it was the passenger ferry, setting out on its daily voyage from Penzance to the Isles of Scilly. It would not pass close enough to be a danger, but its propeller was churning the water and creating a powerful wake. The gleaming white hull towered against the sky, crowned by the orange funnel with its distinctive black-and-white flag emblem . . . then Lizzy noticed that the passengers on deck were pointing at something.

Behind the ship and escorting it with joyful leaps were five dolphins.

'Arhans!' Lizzy screamed with excitement. She knew that the dolphins wouldn't hear her above the noise of the boat's powerful engines, but her despair had turned to hope.

With renewed energy, she started to swim towards her friends. She couldn't hope to catch up with them or the ferry, of course. But it was said that dolphins were telepathic. If it were true, then perhaps they would sense her.

Arhans! Arhans! She concentrated fiercely on repeating the name over and over in her mind. *Arhans, it's me – it's Lizzy! Oh, Arhans!*

Arhans appeared so suddenly out of the churning water ahead that Lizzy whirled backwards in shock. The dolphin streaked towards her, and even above the throbbing of the boat's engines Lizzy could hear her whistling call. She reached Lizzy and swam round her in fast, tight circles, scolding with shrill cries.

'I'm sorry!' Lizzy gasped, dizzy as she tried to follow Arhans's swirling rush. 'I know you told me not to come to the sea, but – Ow! Arhans, that hurt!'

The dolphin had butted her, quite hard, with her snout, and the others arrived and joined in. They all nudged and chivvied Lizzy, their whistles now turning to squeals, and Lizzy realized that they were trying to drive her back towards the shore.

'Stop it, all of you!' she shouted. 'Listen to me, *please*!' Wildly she waved towards the cliffs, though she could no longer see *Silvie*. 'It's my father – he's out there in a boat, and I've *got* to find him!'

Somehow she managed to make herself heard above the dolphins' agitated rebukes, and, as they realized what she was telling them, their noise died down until at last she was able to explain.

'He's borrowed Mr Treleaven's sailing boat, and he's gone to look at the caves down the coast,' she finished. 'I think he's looking for Morvyr. Oh, Arhans, I've *got* to see him and talk to him! Help me, please! Don't make me go back to the shore!'

The dolphins chittered together as if they were conferring about what they should do. Then Arhans swam in close to Lizzy, and one of the others pushed at her hands with its snout, moving them towards Arhans's back. Lizzy understood. They were going to help her reach Jack Carrick. And the fastest way to do it was to take her to him themselves.

Eagerly Lizzy grasped Arhans's dorsal fin with both hands, taking a firm grip. Arhans whistled as though to say, 'Hold tight!' Then with a rush and a plunge they were diving down and away.

Lizzy had ridden on Arhans's back once before when she and Kes had been followed by an unknown enemy and the dolphins had taken her safely to shore. This journey wasn't as wild and exhilarating as that first one had been, but it was still a huge thrill to be towed through the water with the graceful sea creatures swimming beside her. Two dolphins had gone on ahead; after a while, though, Lizzy heard them calling, and moments later their sleek shapes appeared again. They were excited; whistling shrilly, they dived over and under Lizzy and her escort, then they turned again and swam on. Arhans followed, pulling Lizzy with her – then suddenly they all stopped.

Water streamed from Lizzy's hair over her face, and she had to wipe it away before she could see anything. When her eyes cleared, she gasped. The cliffs rose sheer in front of them. And no more than fifty metres away was *Silvie*, her mainsail furled and just her foresail bellying in the wind. Lizzy could see her name painted on her stern. And she could see the man who sat at the tiller. A man with tanned skin, jet-black hair and a beard, dressed in jeans and a salt-bleached denim fisherman's guernsey.

Jack Carrick had his back to the dolphins

and had not yet seen them, and suddenly
Lizzy was hit by a wave of uncertainty. How
could she approach him? What could she
say? She didn't remember him at all, and the
last time he had seen her, she was a tiny
baby. Tears sprang to her eyes. She bit her
lip hard, trying to stop them, but they spilled
down her cheeks and mingled with the sea.
She didn't know what to do! In distress she
pressed her face against Arhans's smooth
side. The dolphins seemed to understand.
They grouped closely round Arhans and
Lizzy – then, catching Lizzy unawares,
Arhans slipped away and headed towards the
bobbing boat. Confused, Lizzy tried to
follow, but the others would not let her.
They surrounded her as though they were
trying to protect and comfort her, and she
could only watch as Arhans swam alongside
Silvie and reared out of the water. Jack
started with surprise, and his voice carried
over the rush and hiss of the tide.

'Ahh!' Then his astonishment turned to eagerness and he reached out towards the dolphin. 'That silver stripe – Arhans, it's you, it's *you*!'

Arhans chittered to him, wagging her head. Jack tensed, then his head whipped round and he looked behind him. His eyes widened – and Lizzy saw that they were the same vivid blue as hers and Kes's.

'*What* –?' He stood up in the boat, staring, his mouth a round O of shock as he saw Lizzy floating between the other four dolphins. The colour drained from his face and he said, '*Morvyr?*'

Lizzy stared back, feeling that her entire world was turning upside down in her head. For a moment she was paralysed. Then, like a taut string breaking, the paralysis snapped.

'N-no . . .' She hardly recognized her own voice. 'I'm Tegenn. Oh, Father – I'm Tegenn!'

Chapter Nine

'Tegenn, Tegenn, I just can't believe it!'
Jack hugged Lizzy tightly to him, his
voice choked. 'After all this time, I've finally
found you!'

They were both in the boat. Jack had
lowered the foresail and dropped the anchor,
and *Silvie* bobbed gently, close to the cliffs
where the water was quieter. The dolphins
had gathered round them and were happily
watching the reunion, nodding their heads
and making odd little creaking sounds that
seemed to express their delight.

At last Jack released Lizzy and they both

sat back, breathless. 'There's so much to tell you!' Lizzy was so overcome with excitement and emotion that she was almost babbling. 'I was found abandoned, and I was adopted and taken away, but then we moved here, and I met Kes and . . .' She took a huge gulping breath as the words ran out. 'I'm not making much sense, am I? I just don't know where to start!'

She was laughing and crying at the same time, and Jack laughed too. 'It doesn't matter!' he said. 'We've got all the time we want now. Let me look at you again.' He took hold of her shoulders and gazed at her with shining eyes. 'You're so pretty. You look just like your mother.'

'Do I?' Lizzy felt a warm glow. 'I think she's the most beautiful person I've ever seen.'

He smiled. 'So do I. I've missed you all so much! Has it really been eleven years since I went away?'

Lizzy nodded. 'Kes says you went to search for me.'

'I did. When you were stolen, we believed you'd been taken far across the sea.' Jack frowned. 'The person who stole you laid a false trail, because she thought that if I were out of the way –'

Lizzy interrupted quickly. '*She?* You mean . . . Taran?'

He frowned. 'Do you know about that?'

'I know about *her*,' Lizzy said fiercely. 'Kes told me that she's wicked and cruel, and hasn't got the right to be Queen at all. But he doesn't know any more, because Morvyr – Mother – won't talk about it.'

'She's right not to. But now I'm back, things can be different.' Jack looked around at the sea. 'Where are your mother and brother now? Are they nearby? I so much want to see them!'

Amid all the excitement Lizzy hadn't had a chance to tell him about Morvyr and Kes's disappearance. Quickly she described her encounter with the giant eel when she was searching for Kes, and how the dolphins had intervened and driven him away.

'Arhans tried to explain what had happened, but I haven't learned to understand her properly yet. There was a word I sort of picked up . . . Tull-something, or Toll . . . '

Jack's eyes narrowed. 'Tullor?'

'Yes! That was it – Tullor.'

'Ah, so *he's* still around, is he? I might have guessed.'

'Do you know him?' Lizzy asked uneasily.

'Oh, yes. He's Taran's most trusted servant, and as evil a creature as you could wish *not* to meet. Thank goodness Arhans and the others found you in time!' Jack was frowning deeply now. 'Did you understand anything else that Arhans said?'

'I know she was warning me to stay away from the sea – and I think she said Morvyr and Kes are in hiding for some reason. I don't know why, or where they've gone, but I'm sure they're in danger!'

Before Jack could reply, Arhans swam up to the boat and whistled urgently. Jack frowned at her. 'What's that, Arhans?' The dolphin whistled again and he shook his head. 'It's been so long since I've tried to talk to her; I'm not sure . . . but I think she's saying that Taran has ordered Morvyr and Kes to be arrested!'

'*Arrested?*' Lizzy was horrified. 'Why? What have they done?'

'I don't know. But I've got an idea . . .' Suddenly he swung to face Lizzy again. 'Tegenn, when you were a baby, you had a mother-of-pearl locket. Do you know what happened to it?'

'I've still got it,' said Lizzy. 'It was round my neck when I was found abandoned.'

'Where is it now?'

'At home. Morvyr told me never to wear it when I go to the sea.'

He nodded slowly. 'Good. Then, with luck, it's not too late . . .' He turned again. 'Arhans, do you know where Morvyr and Kes are?'

Arhans chittered eagerly and tossed her head.

'Can you take a message to them without Taran or her servants knowing?'

The dolphins seemed to confer together, then Arhans whistled what Lizzy thought was agreement.

'All right. Then tell them that I've come home and I've found Tegenn. Ask Morvyr if she can meet me somewhere – anywhere – and, if that's not safe, bring word to me from her. Will you do that?'

Arhans whistled again. Jack reached out and stroked her back. 'Thank you! And, Arhans – tell her that the ninth one is still safe with me!'

Lizzy was puzzled by these last words, but Arhans seemed to understand. She and the other dolphins turned in the water with flicks of their powerful tails and surged away. Jack and Lizzy watched until they were out of sight, then Jack sighed.

'All we can do now is wait,' he said.

'Will the dolphins find them, do you think?'

'Yes, they will. Arhans knows where they are, and she says it's a safe place where Taran and her henchmen would never think of looking – not even Tullor.'

Lizzy shivered. 'If the dolphins hadn't rescued me from Tullor, what would he have done?'

'My guess is that Taran had ordered him to capture you and take you to her.'

'But why? What could she possibly want with me?'

'That's easy to answer. She wanted you as a hostage.'

Lizzy's eyes widened as she began to understand. 'You mean, she'd have used me to make Morvyr and Kes come out of hiding?'

'Exactly. Because, you see, she thinks that one of you has got something she wants. And maybe she's right.'

'Wh-what is it?'

'It's –' Then Jack stopped. 'No. It isn't safe to talk about it here.' He glanced uneasily towards the cliffs. 'You can never be sure whether someone might be listening. Tegenn, I think we should go back now. Come with me in the boat. I'll take you to shore, then we'll meet again tomorrow –'

'Tomorrow?' Lizzy said, aghast. 'I can't wait till then!'

He shook his head. 'You must, little one.' He blinked and his face grew sad. 'Because we've got to keep our secret, haven't we? We can't just go back to the town and tell everyone that I'm your real father. It wouldn't be fair.' He gave her a wry smile. 'They probably wouldn't believe it anyway.'

Lizzy realized he was right. Slowly, reluctantly, she nodded.

'Don't fret,' said Jack. 'Tomorrow'll come soon enough. And then I'll have something to show you. Something very important. Now, try and cheer up! I'll teach you a bit about sailing on the way back, if you like. And you can tell me all the things I don't know about you!'

By the time the boat approached the marina, Jack Carrick knew most of Lizzy's story: how she had been found abandoned as a baby and adopted by the Baxters, who had taken her away to live in another part of the country. There was one bad moment, though, when Lizzy was explaining about the family's move to Cornwall. 'They'd always wanted to live here, then Dad was offered a teaching job at –' She stopped in sudden dismay as she realized what she had said. 'I mean, he – Mr Baxter – I've always called him Dad, you see –'

'Of course you have, and so you should,'

said Jack gently. 'He's the only dad you've known until now, Tegenn. That won't change. It can't.'

His eyes were sad and Lizzy felt tears welling. 'I'm not even called Tegenn any more,' she confessed in a small voice. 'They named me Elizabeth. Lizzy. I only found out my real name when I met Kes.'

'Then Lizzy it'll be,' said Jack. 'I like it, anyway. It suits you.' He saw her face and smiled. 'Don't worry. We've both got a lot to get used to. But we can do it, can't we? Now, tell me all about that first meeting with Kes . . .'

The outboard engine chugged gently as Jack steered *Silvie* into her berth on the pontoons.

'Make her fast,' he said to Lizzy, and watched as she tied and secured the mooring rope with the knot – a Fisherman's Hitch, he called it – that he'd taught her on the way home. 'Very professional!' he added with a grin when she finished. 'You'll be a proper sailor before you know it!'

Lizzy smiled back, pleased by his praise. She wished they could have stayed out at sea all day. There was so much still to talk about – she hadn't heard anything of *his* story yet – and she just wanted to be with him, and enjoy getting to know him for the very first time.

Jack jumped ashore and held out his hand to help Lizzy. As she stepped from the boat, a familiar voice called cheerfully, 'Hi, Mr Carrick! So my sister managed to meet you, did she? You sneaky thing, Lizzy!'

'Hello, Rose – hello, Paul.' Jack smiled as Rose sauntered up, with Paul a few paces behind her. 'Yes, Teg– Lizzy and I have met. In fact we're already getting to be like old friends.'

'What did you do, fish her out of the sea?' Rose joked.

'That's about it. Just like a mermaid.' He winked at Lizzy, and Lizzy flushed scarlet.

Luckily Rose didn't notice. 'Honestly, she's been so curious about you – she even wanted to come with me to Paul's yesterday. Hope she hasn't been asking loads of nosy questions!' She raised her eyebrows at Lizzy, who turned even redder and looked away.

'We saw *Silvie* coming in,' said Paul, 'so we came down to meet you. Rose wants to try her hand at sailing. I said I'd take her out for a bit, if you don't want the boat any more.'

Jack was still smiling. He was so calm and quick-thinking, Lizzy thought; Rose surely wouldn't be suspicious. 'Good for you, Rose,' he said. 'Well, enjoy yourselves. I'll see you later, Paul.'

'OK.' Paul helped Rose into the boat, and Jack and Lizzy walked away.

'Thanks,' said Lizzy after a few moments. 'When I saw Rose, I didn't know what to do.' She looked up at Jack. 'It's going to be hard when I get home. I've got to pretend not to be excited.'

'I know, love. But you can do it. After all, you haven't told anyone about Kes and Morvyr, have you?'

'No-o . . . But this is different, somehow. They live in the sea, but you're *here*. And if we meet when there are other people around, like just now, it's so hard to act as if you're no one special.'

He nodded. 'It's hard for me too. But we've got to keep the secret, Lizzy. You understand why, don't you?'

She nodded, blinking. 'I couldn't tell Mum and Dad – I mean, them – the Baxt–'

'Shh! "Mum and Dad" is fine, I told you that. No, of course you can't tell them. It wouldn't be fair on them, or you. Now, listen: we've still got a lot to say to each other – and there are things you don't know that I need to tell you. Let's meet up tomorrow.' He paused. 'Have you got any favourite places that you like to go to?'

Lizzy thought. 'The headland where the lighthouse is,' she said.

'That's good; it's quiet, and it's on land. That's important – I'll explain why tomorrow. How about having a picnic lunch there?'

'Yes!' said Lizzy eagerly. 'That would be great!'

'All right. Say, half past twelve, then. I'll bring the picnic. And I want you to wear your locket.' She looked at him curiously, but he put a finger to his lips. 'No more now. I'd better get back to the Treleavens'. See you tomorrow – and maybe Arhans will have some news for us by then.'

He touched her arm lightly and hurried away. Lizzy watched as he walked past the lifeboat station. There he paused, looked back and waved. She waved too. And she continued to watch until he was out of sight.

Chapter Ten

Kes was starting to wonder how long he could bear the inactivity and the tension. Though he and Morvyr had only been in hiding for a few days, it felt like ages. And until they knew that it was safe, Morvyr said they must not leave.

'But how *will* we know?' he had asked her in frustration. 'We might stay here all the rest of the summer and never be sure!'

'The dolphins will bring word to us,' said his mother. 'Queen Taran's sure to give up the search eventually and find something else to amuse her. When she does, Arhans will soon hear about it.'

Kes couldn't argue. But the cave where they were living now felt like a prison. For one thing, it was miles from their home cave, right out near Land's End. It was much smaller too; there was only one room, with none of the furnishings and trappings that made theirs so pleasant. It was deep in the cliffs, and very gloomy, the only light coming through a split in the rocks that allowed them to glimpse just a tiny strip of sky high above. Worst of all, Kes felt completely cut off, for instead of simply swimming through a seaweed curtain, you had to feel your way through a long, narrow and pitch-dark fissure to reach the outside world. Not that he could go outside anyway. Neither of them could. Arhans had warned them that it was too dangerous to venture beyond the cave entrance. It was even risky for the dolphins to visit them unless absolutely necessary.

Instead, they sent various sea creatures, small enough not to attract the attention of Taran's spies, to bring them food and any news. But crabs, lobsters and fish didn't make very interesting companions. Kes was desperately bored. And he couldn't stop thinking and worrying about Lizzy.

So when he heard Arhans's whistling call echoing hollowly through the fissure tunnel, his heart gave a huge lurch under his ribs.

'Mother –' He grasped Morvyr's arm.

'I heard! It must be something vitally important – something she can't entrust to one of the other creatures . . .'

Moments later Arhans emerged from the tunnel, which was just big enough for her to squeeze through. She whistled again, urgently – and Kes and Morvyr's eyes widened in shock as they realized what she was telling them.

'He's back . . .?' Morvyr's voice was a

whisper, and all the colour had drained from her face. 'My Jack – he's really come back?'

Kes had hardly ever seen his mother cry before. There were rainbow colours in Morvyr's tears, and they flowed away and mingled with the water in the undersea cave. Concerned, Arhans nudged and nuzzled at her, and at last her sobs changed to a hiccupping laugh.

'It's all right, Arhans. I'm crying because I'm *happy*! Tell me, please – tell me everything you know!'

With growing excitement she and Kes listened to the whole story, including the tale of Lizzy's meeting with Jack out at sea. Arhans gave them Jack's message, and Morvyr, who was calm again now, said, 'If only we could go to him!' Immediately Arhans started to protest and she added, 'I know, I know – we mustn't leave this cave until Taran calls off the search for us. But oh, Arhans, couldn't you bring Jack here in his boat? I so much want to see him!'

Arhans wasn't happy with that idea, either. If Taran also knew that Jack had returned, she would have set spies to watch for him in the hope that he would lead them to Morvyr. It was too dangerous, Arhans said. They would just have to be patient. But, in the meantime, she added, Jack had given her one more message for Morvyr. He had said: 'Tell her the ninth one is still safe with me.'

Morvyr gave a shocked gasp. 'The ninth . . .? Oh!'

'Mother?' Kes frowned at her. 'What does that mean?'

Morvyr wouldn't meet his curious stare. 'Arhans,' she said. 'Go back to Jack. Tell him I understand. And say . . .' She hesitated. 'No. That will keep. Just say that Kes and I are here, and we're waiting.'

Arhans needed to breathe soon, so, after promising to return in a few days, she left them, wriggling back into the fissure and

vanishing in the darkness. When she had
gone, there was silence for some moments.
Then Kes couldn't bear it any longer and
blurted, 'Mother, I don't understand! "The
ninth one" – what *is* it?'

Morvyr turned to him, her eyes very
serious, and put her hands on his shoulders.
'Please, Kes,' she said, 'don't ask me about it
now. I can't tell you yet. But when we see
your father, I'll explain everything. I
promise.'

Kes knew from her tone of voice that he
wouldn't persuade her to change her mind,
so he asked no more questions. But Arhans's
incredible news brought his nerves close to
breaking point. He wanted to go straight out
of the cave, through the fissure to the open
sea, then swim and swim and swim until he
reached the fishing port and found his father.
He knew it would be wrong, dangerous,
stupid, but the urge was so strong that it
hurt.

He tried to distract himself by helping
Morvyr to prepare their meal. When it was
ready, though, he could hardly eat anything.
A shoal of tiny fish had swum into the cave
and were darting all around the walls, but
Kes couldn't even summon up enough
interest to play their favourite chasing game
with them. He tried again to talk to his
mother, but she barely seemed to hear, and
he realized that she was as keyed up as he
was. At last, not knowing what else he could
do that was bearable, Kes lay down on the
seaweed-covered rock ledge that served as his
bed, and fell asleep.

When he woke, the dull daylight in the
cave had faded to an even dimmer silver-
grey. It must be night, he realized, and the
silver-grey was the light of the moon. Peering
into the gloom he saw his mother lying on
another ledge with a slow trickle of bubbles
rising from her mouth. Kes drifted carefully
and quietly towards her. Her breathing was

even and he thought she was asleep. But then he saw her eyes gleaming in the darkness, and a moment later she sat up.

'Oh, Kes.' Her voice sounded strained. 'I can't sleep.'

'Me too.' He took hold of her outstretched hand. 'Knowing that Father's come home but we can't see him . . . Mother, how long are we going to have to wait? I don't *want* to wait. This is too important!'

Morvyr did not answer, but eased herself from the ledge and swam slowly across the cave. At last she said, 'I was thinking . . . It's night. Even Queen Taran's servants have to sleep sometimes. Besides, the darkness would hide us . . .' Her words trailed off and Kes felt his heartbeat getting faster.

'You mean – go *now*? And find Father?' He stopped and swallowed as a huge surge of excitement constricted his chest.

'We could reach the harbour by morning,' said Morvyr, her voice not quite steady. 'And then you could go to shore and ask Lizzy to tell him . . .'

'Yes, Mother, yes! Oh, please, let's do it!' He flung a glance towards the fissure that led out of the cave. He could hear the sea surging, but it was quieter and calmer than it had been for the past few days. 'We can find the way in the dark, can't we? And you're right, no one could see us the way they would in daylight!'

'I don't know . . . If anything went wrong . . .' Morvyr started to swim round in circles. Her tail flicked agitatedly, and Kes knew that she was wavering. Desperately he tried to persuade her.

'Nothing will go wrong!' he said. 'And once we're close to shore we'll be safe, because anything big enough to harm us won't dare go into such shallow water. It's our chance, Mother, maybe our only one. We've *got* to do it!'

For a few seconds longer Morvyr

continued to swim in circles. Then she
slowed down, stopped and looked at Kes.
Her storm-grey eyes were shining brilliantly,
and her face was set with determination.

'All right,' she said. 'We *will* do it. We'll
do it together.'

They said nothing as they swam to the
tunnel. At the entrance Kes looked back, but
the large brown crab that shared the cave
with them had disappeared into its favourite
crevice and wasn't watching. His heart was
beating fast with a mixture of excitement
and fear, but he firmly thrust the fear away.
They were going to find his father. That was
all that mattered!

Morvyr grasped his hand briefly and
squeezed it. Then, stretching their arms out
in front of them like divers, they surged into
the tunnel.

Though moonlight was filtering down
through the water, Kes could only see a

metre or two around him. Morvyr was a
dimly shining shape just ahead. Every so
often the pale oval of her face showed as she
looked over her shoulder to make sure he
was following closely, but her features were a
blur.

The journey wasn't easy. Several times they
had to swerve to avoid rocks that loomed
suddenly and unexpectedly in their path, and
once Kes's swerve was too late and he grazed
his arm painfully on the barnacle-covered
surface. After that, Morvyr signalled that
they should slow down. It was frustrating,
but better than risking worse injury.

They hadn't spoken since they left the
cave, but communicated only with hand
signals, moving silently on through the water.
Apart from a few curious fish that came to
look at them they saw no other creatures.
That didn't mean they weren't there, of
course, but if he couldn't see them, Kes
reasoned, chances were they couldn't see

him. That was a comforting thought. He didn't even want to meet any of the dolphins. They would only make them go back to the cave, and Kes was determined that they would reach their goal. They were making good progress. It couldn't be too far now.

When he first had the feeling that they were being followed, he tried to ignore it. In the strange world of undersea night it was easy to imagine all kinds of strange things, and if he let it get the better of him, he would lose his nerve. So he swam on behind Morvyr. Occasionally he looked over his shoulder, just in case, but he saw nothing.

Until, as they passed a massive rock with a jagged tip that rose above the water, something reared up from the gloom and lunged at them.

Kes screamed with shock and fright – and it was the worst thing he could have done, for the scream sent a surge of bubbles streaming up from his mouth and in front of his face. For one vital second he couldn't see. Then, before the bubbles could clear, a long tentacle snaked round his tail and gripped it.

'*No!*' Kes lashed his tail frantically, but whatever had got hold of him held on. As he struggled to get away, another tentacle shot out and wrapped round his left arm.

Another scream rang out and Kes yelled, '*Mother!*' Two shapes were writhing in the water a short way off, struggling together – he thought one of them was Morvyr but couldn't see anything clearly. Desperately he twisted round – and screamed again as he found himself face to face with a monstrous shape that pulsed with vivid, ever-changing colours. Cold, bulbous eyes glared at him, and he realized that his attacker was a cuttlefish. But he had never seen such a giant one in his life – it was as big as he was, and far stronger. Now the eight tentacles that grew from its hideous head came writhing towards him; four pinned his own arms to his sides while the others took a tighter hold of his tail. He could feel the power of the suckers on the thing's arms, and with horror he realized he was helpless.

'*Mother!*' he yelled again. Where was she? He couldn't see her now – had she, too, been caught?

Then, from the darkness, a voice said, 'Well done, my friends.'

Vivid lines of blue and green pulsed along the cuttlefish's body, as though it was excited by the praise. With a huge effort Kes craned over his shoulder, and saw a bigger, darker shape undulating out from behind the rock.

Tullor opened his mouth, showing his savage teeth. 'Well, Kesson. So you and your mother have come out from your hiding place, have you? I wonder what could be important enough to make you do that?'

Kes tried not to show how scared he was. 'Where's my mother?' he demanded, trying not to let his voice quaver. 'What have you done to her?'

'Nothing that she won't recover from soon enough.' Tullor swam slowly round him, like a hunter sizing up its prey. 'So, we have found both of you. How very gratifying. The Queen will be pleased.'

'I'm not scared of the Queen!' Kes lied defiantly.

The cuttlefish's colour changed to purple again, pulsing faster than ever. Tullor uttered another snarl that sounded like a warning.

'No!' he snapped. 'Remember your instructions – he is not to be harmed!' Still swimming in slow circles, he stared at Kes until Kes couldn't stand it any longer and looked away. 'Mmm . . .' The sound was part hiss and part growl. 'You are a stubborn child, Kesson – and to pretend you're not afraid of the Queen is very foolish. So, we will take you to a place where you can learn some sense.' He showed his teeth again. 'A place where none of your friends will ever find you.'

'No!' Kes shouted. 'I won't go with you! You can't make me!'

'Oh, we can. Because, you see, if you try to fight us, we will hurt your mother.'

He turned his head and hissed into the darkness. Moments later something came swimming towards them, and Kes drew in his breath sharply. Another cuttlefish, as big as the first – and grasped in its tentacles was Morvyr. Her arms and tail hung limply; her eyes were closed. She was unconscious.

'Her safety depends on you, Kesson,' said Tullor unpleasantly. 'Do you understand?'

Kes did, and tears sprang to his eyes. He blinked them back and said nothing.

'That's better.' Tullor was almost purring with satisfaction. He looked at the cuttlefish. 'Let's not waste any more time.'

With a wriggle of his tail he swam off. The cuttlefish pulsed eagerly once more, and its grip tightened. Then, with a surge of energy, it hurtled away through the water at astounding speed, dragging Kes with it. The second cuttlefish did the same, with Morvyr in its grip, and the two of them followed Tullor into the darkness of the open sea.

Half a lifetime seemed to pass as Kes was towed on and on, towards an unknown destination.

He could no longer see Morvyr and her captor. Buffeted by currents, numb where the suckered tentacles gripped him, he was too dizzy and sick and exhausted to be aware of anything but the rushing journey. And still it showed no signs of ending.

At last, though, he realized that their headlong pace was slowing down. He had shut his eyes in an effort to drive away the sickness; now with a great effort he forced them to open.

He knew at once that they were a long

way from land. This was the truly deep sea –
green-black and mysterious and menacing.
He had never been this far out before, and
he felt bewildered, lost and afraid. He
couldn't see the seabed or the surface; they
were both too far away. All he could make
out was the cuttlefish's bulky body above
him, fins flapping like wings as it swam, and
ahead of it the dark, snakelike shape of
Tullor leading the way. But where to?

They were still slowing down, and
suddenly he heard Tullor's rasping voice.

'We are almost there. The indigo gateway
is just below us – bring the captives.'

With a jerk that seemed to rattle Kes's
teeth the cuttlefish twisted and dived
downwards. Kes could feel the pressure in
his ears increasing, he could hardly breathe,
he was gasping –

Then he saw the rock looming towards
him from below. It was huge, and peculiarly
round as though it wasn't natural but had

been cut into shape. There was a dip in the
centre, like a pool. Tullor swam to the dip
and hovered in the water above it. He waited
. . . then to Kes's shock, a voice that seemed
to come from inside the hollow whispered,

'*Who is there?*'

The cuttlefish writhed, and the bands of
colour chasing each other along its body
brightened with excitement. Then the eel
said, 'It is Tullor. Brath and Hager are with
me – we have Morvyr and the boy!'

'*Ah!*' There was delight and a horrible
kind of triumph in the eerie voice. '*Enter!*'

The water in the hollow started to swirl
like a whirlpool, and Kes's eyes widened as a
strange purplish-blue light appeared in its
depths. The light brightened, illuminating
Tullor's cruel face. He wriggled towards it
and the cuttlefish followed, pulling Kes
along. Kes struggled, but there was nothing
he could do. Then as they reached the
hollow the light flared blindingly – he had a

sensation of falling, falling, and yelled in terror as he plunged into a spinning tunnel.

'No! Let go of me! I won't, I won't, I – *OHH*!'

Kes's shouts broke off in a yell of astonishment as he surfaced in a brightly lit circular cave. The light was dazzling after the dark sea, and he blinked, shaking water from his eyes and trying to make out where he was.

The first things he saw were the mirrors. There were nine of them round the cave wall, all glowing with light. Seven were the seven colours of the rainbow: red, orange, yellow, green, blue, indigo and violet; the eighth was silver, and the ninth was black. Their surfaces rippled as though they were made of water rather than glass, and there were dim reflections in the seven rainbow mirrors, though the silver and black ones showed nothing at all.

He jumped with shock as, behind him, someone laughed.

Flailing, he tried to turn round and see who was there. But the cuttlefish, Brath, renewed its grip and he couldn't move. The unseen person laughed again. Then a beautiful silvery voice said,

'Sleep!'

Kes gasped as a tingling sensation flooded through his mind and body. He tried to fight it, but it was too powerful. The scene was fading . . . he felt as if he were falling again . . .

His eyes closed and he slumped unconscious in the water.

Chapter Eleven

Lizzy had been in a state of high excitement all morning at the prospect of her meeting with Jack. Unable to wait any longer, she left home half an hour early and ran through the streets and then along the cliff path. As she approached the lighthouse she saw a familiar figure outlined against the blue sky. Her heart skipped eagerly. The figure saw her, waved and then sprinted the last fifty metres to her.

'Hello, Lizzy!' Jack Carrick enveloped her in a hug that lifted her off her feet.

'Hello, D–!' Lizzy was about to say 'Dad'

but stopped. She had called Morvyr
'Mother', but this was different. She was on
land. Jack Carrick was an ordinary human
being. Somehow it was all too close to home,
and she was confused. As he put her down
she blinked and said, 'I don't know what to
call you . . .'

'Well, not Mr Carrick, for a start!' he
replied with a grin. 'And, to be honest, I
don't think it should be Dad, either, do you?'

She looked crestfallen. 'Not even just
between us?'

He shook his head. 'Better not. What if
you said it in front of someone? We'd have
some explaining to do, and I don't think
your family – your human family – is ready
for the truth just yet.'

Lizzy nodded. 'Yes, I – I see what you
mean. What *shall* I say, then?'

'How about just plain Jack? That's what
my friends call me. And we're friends above
all, aren't we?'

Lizzy returned a hesitant smile. 'All right, then . . . Jack.'

'Good for you! Right, let's find a nice spot for this picnic I've brought, then we can make ourselves comfortable and talk.'

They chose a sunny patch of grass that was sheltered from the sea wind by the bulk of the lighthouse, and sat down. Jack had brought pasties, salad, lemonade and a chunk of a magnificent chocolate cake made by Mrs Treleaven. Chocolate cake was one of Lizzy's favourite things on earth; she just hoped that she wouldn't be too excited to eat.

'I've got some good news,' said Jack as they unpacked the food. 'I went to the beach early this morning, and Arhans was there. She's seen your mother and Kes, and given them my message.'

Lizzy's eyes lit up. 'That's brilliant! Did she tell you where they are?'

'Yes. But she warned me not to go there.

Taran has so many spies, and we can't take the risk of leading them to the hiding place. We'll have to be patient for a while longer.' He saw her face and smiled sympathetically. 'It's hard for me too, but at least we know they're safe. In the meantime we've got a lot more to talk about. And the most important thing is your locket. Did you bring it with you?'

'Yes.' The locket was round her neck, and Lizzy drew it out from under her T-shirt. Jack stared at it, then nodded. 'Do you know about the secret compartment, Lizzy?'

She swallowed. 'Yes. Mother – I mean, Morvyr – showed it to me. I'd never realized it was there.'

'Did she open it for you?'

Lizzy nodded. Her pulse was pounding.

'And . . .?'

'There's a pearl inside it. A silver pearl.' She hesitated. 'Morvyr touched it and – and said, "Sing." And . . . it did . . .'

Jack was smiling now. 'May I see it?' he asked.

Lizzy's hands shook as she took off the locket, unfastened the catch and ran her fingers gently over the inside surface. She didn't know how Morvyr had made the secret compartment work; there must be a knack to it, but she hadn't watched closely enough –

She jumped in surprise and almost dropped the locket as, with a faint *click*, the inner compartment sprang open. The beautiful silver pearl was there, shimmering in the bright sunlight.

Jack gazed at the pearl for a few moments. Then he said, 'Touch it, Lizzy, and tell it to sing.'

She reached out and touched the pearl very gently. 'Sing,' she whispered.

The pearl began to give off the high, sweet note that she had heard before. Then suddenly a second note joined in, as sweet as the first but deeper.

Startled, Lizzy looked up at Jack. 'It didn't do that before!' she said. 'That second note – what is it?'

Jack smiled. 'This.'

He reached to his own neck, and drew out a mother-of-pearl locket exactly like her own.

'I made them for you and Kes when you were born,' he said. 'This one has a secret compartment too – look.'

To Lizzy's delight a tiny section of Jack's locket opened. Inside was another shining pearl. But where Lizzy's pearl was silver, this one was deepest black – and the black pearl was also singing.

Lizzy gasped in astonishment as the sounds of the two singing pearls grew louder and louder, until the air was filled with a beautiful harmony.

'Better close them away now, before anyone else hears them,' said Jack. He shut his locket, and reluctantly Lizzy did the same. Slowly the singing faded, then it was gone, leaving only the sounds of the sea and the wind.

Lizzy looked up at Jack. 'Wh-what does it mean?' she asked in a whisper.

'These two pearls have a very special link,' Jack replied. 'When one of them sings, the other answers, and if it isn't far away the first pearl "hears" it and echoes its voice. The closer they are, the louder the singing becomes.' He smiled. 'When you were stolen I hoped that the black pearl would help me to find you, so I took it with me in the locket I'd made for Kes.' He gave a little laugh. 'I must have sailed three times round the world in the last eleven years, and every day I asked the black pearl to sing. But the silver pearl never sang in reply.'

'Because they were too far away from each other?'

'Yes. But not long ago I arrived in Brittany – how I got there is much too long a story

to tell now – and, when I asked the black
pearl to sing, I heard the silver pearl too. It
was very faint, but it was there. I knew I
was getting close to you at long last. I went
to a fishing port on the coast, and I listened
again. This time the silver pearl's voice was
stronger, and I had a feeling that I must
come back to Cornwall.'

'That's why you were on the French
trawler!'

Jack nodded. 'And you know what
happened after that.'

Lizzy looked out to sea. She was thinking
about the lifeboat rescue, and how nearly
Jack had been lost forever. She swallowed.
'There's still so much I don't know, though,'
she said at last. 'What *are* the pearls? Where
did they come from? And why is Morvyr so
afraid of anyone knowing about them?'

'Ah, that's the other part of the story.' Jack
looked around to see if anyone else was
nearby. There were some people on the cliff

path, but they were too far away to overhear anything, and he continued.

'These pearls were once part of the mermaid Queen's crown. There are nine of them altogether, and they all have their own magic. But the black and silver pearls are the most magical of all. If they are ever restored to their proper place, whoever wears the crown will have enormous power.'

'Is it Taran's crown?' Lizzy asked.

'Taran has it now. But Kes is right; she isn't the true Queen. She's a usurper. Whatever happens, the black and silver pearls must be kept out of her clutches. That's why your mother told you not to take your locket to sea. Taran would do anything to get her hands on those two pearls and make the crown complete again. If she knew you had one, you'd be in great danger.'

Lizzy felt a shiver go through her at the thought.

'Taran was always a troublemaker,' Jack

went on. 'She was jealous and ambitious. She wanted to be Queen, and she was determined to get her way at any cost. So eleven years ago she gathered a group of followers – creatures as greedy and unscrupulous as herself – and they planned to attack the true Queen, Kara, and steal her magical crown.

'The attack took Queen Kara completely by surprise. None of her loyal people were close by. When they realized what was happening, they went to the rescue, but by then it was too late. Taran got away, and they found Kara lying badly wounded in her undersea home.'

Jack's eyes became misty. 'Kara told them that Taran had stolen the crown and kidnapped her daughter, Karwynna. Everyone was horrified, because the nine pearls in the crown give great power to whoever wears it. But Taran didn't have all the pearls. During the struggle Queen Kara managed to prise two of them free.'

'The silver one and the black one . . .'
Lizzy breathed.

'Yes. Taran and her henchmen fled without
them when the loyal merfolk arrived. The
Queen entrusted the pearls to Morvyr, and
Morvyr promised that, if they could, she and
her friends would somehow find a way to
defeat Taran and restore the crown to the
rightful heir.' He paused. 'A few minutes
later, Queen Kara died.'

Lizzy felt a choking mixture of sadness and
anger. Tears stung the backs of her eyes and
she had to bite her lip in an effort to stop
them from falling.

Jack understood, and reached out to
squeeze her hand. 'Your mother hid the pearls
in your lockets and sealed them with
protective magic,' he went on gently. 'Taran
proclaimed herself Queen a few days later,
and even with only seven pearls the crown
gave her great power. But she wanted the
black and silver pearls too. They're the most

powerful of all, and if she could get her hands on them, she would be almost invincible.'

'Did she know where they were?'

'Not for certain. She suspected that Queen Kara had given them to your mother, but she couldn't do anything about it because I was there.' Jack's eyes glinted angrily. 'I wasn't afraid of Taran, and she knew it.'

Lizzy was beginning to understand. 'So that's why she kidnapped me! She wanted to lure you away, so that there was no one to protect Morvyr!'

'That's right. She laid a false trail that made us think you'd been taken far across the sea, and I followed the trail to search for you.'

'But what about Taran? Weren't you afraid of what she'd do to Morvyr if you weren't there?'

Jack shook his head. 'We both knew she wouldn't do anything. She could search every cranny of our home, but she wouldn't find the pearls, because they were hidden in the lockets. You were wearing yours when you were stolen, and I took Kes's with me.'

'Taran must have been furious!'

'I'm sure she was. But if she harmed Morvyr she'd never find out where the pearls had gone. So we knew your mother would be safe.'

Lizzy nodded. 'And now,' she said musingly, 'we've both come home, and so have the pearls.' She looked up. 'Do you think we can make Morvyr's promise to Queen Kara come true?'

Jack smiled at her. 'Is that what you'd like?'

Lizzy didn't hesitate. 'Yes,' she said. 'More than anything.'

They walked home an hour later. The picnic had hardly been touched, which was a shame, but neither Lizzy nor Jack could think about food while so much else was on their minds. Lizzy felt as if her head were whirling. She had learned so many things, and all of them so astonishing, that she could hardly begin to take it all in. Only one thought was becoming clearer and clearer. They *must* find a way to defeat Taran and restore the mermaid Queen's crown to Karwynna, the rightful heir.

She looked at Jack as he walked along beside her and said, 'Where do you think Queen Kara's daughter is now?'

'Karwynna?' Jack shook his head. 'I wish I knew, Lizzy. But nobody does. Taran kidnapped her when she attacked the Queen, and Arhans says that nothing's been heard of her since then.' He frowned. 'We don't even know if she's still alive.'

'You think Taran *killed* her?'

'I wouldn't put anything past her.' He looked at Lizzy, his eyes suddenly serious. 'And that's why I want you to be very careful when you go into the sea. Yesterday, for instance – it was wonderful to meet you like that, but you shouldn't have done it. Until we know more about what Taran's up to, you could be in danger.'

Lizzy nodded soberly. 'I understand that now. I'm sorry.'

'Well, there was no harm done, thankfully. But in future make sure the dolphins are with you. Creatures like Tullor won't try anything while they're around.'

They were nearing the harbour now, where they would go their separate ways: Lizzy to her home and Jack to the Treleavens'. When they reached the road, Jack stopped.

'I won't be here for the next day or so,' he said, then saw Lizzy's expression and added, 'It's nothing to worry about! Jeff Treleaven is taking his fishing boat to sea early tomorrow morning, and I'm going along as extra crew.' He smiled. 'It'll be good to be back at work again.'

'Even after what happened to the French trawler?' Lizzy asked in surprise.

'Oh, yes! When the sea's in your blood, you can't stay away from it for long, no matter what.'

'When are you coming back?' Lizzy didn't want him to go, though she tried to keep the disappointment from her voice.

'Oh, we'll only be away two or three days. Rose will soon know; Paul's coming too, and they're sure to be constantly texting each other!'

Lizzy laughed. 'And when you are back,' she said, 'maybe it'll be safe for Kes and Morvyr to come out of hiding.'

'Let's hope so. Oh – I nearly forgot. I've got something for you.' He dug in a pocket and gave her a piece of folded paper. 'When Taran usurped the throne, the merfolk made a rhyme. They used to whisper it to each other as a sign of their belief that Taran's rule won't last forever. No one dares say it now. But I remembered it, and I wrote it down for you.'

Lizzy unfolded the paper. The verse on it was quite short:

> *Red is the sunrise, Orange the sky,*
> *Golden the shimmering sand.*
> *Green are the pools where the small*
>   *fishes lie,*
> *Blue water rolls to the land.*
> *Indigo shadows hide secrets in caves,*
> *Violet the glow of the night.*
> *But Silver and Black will call them*
>   *all back*
> *When a terrible wrong is put right.*

She looked up, blinking. 'It's lovely.'

'It is, isn't it? And let's hope it comes true.' Suddenly he bent and kissed her forehead. 'Take care, Lizzy. I'll be back again soon.'

'Can I come and see you off tomorrow?'

'Of course you can – that would be good. See you then!'

Lizzy watched as he walked away. She thought about the rhyme and what it meant. *But Silver and Black will call them all back, When a terrible wrong is put right . . .*

Carefully she folded the piece of paper until it was as small as she could make it, opened her locket and placed the paper carefully inside. Then, with one last look at Jack's retreating figure, she turned and headed towards her home.

Chapter Twelve

Kes woke up sluggishly and rolled over in the water, yawning and feeling muzzy-headed. He was glad to wake, because he'd been having a nightmare. In it he was swimming at night with his mother, and they had been attacked by . . . by . . .

A jolt went through him as his mind cleared and he remembered. It hadn't been a nightmare at all – it was *real*!

His eyes snapped open and he stared around.

This wasn't the open sea – and it wasn't night. There was a strange glow all around him, a bit like sunlight but yellower and . . . *thicker* was the only word he could think of. It made everything hazy and dim, as if he were swimming in milk rather than water. There was something in front of him, a vague, undulating image – Kes swam towards it, and to his surprise bumped into a wall as solid and smooth and hard as glass.

He peered through, trying to see what was on the other side, but the thick yellow light made it difficult. There was something that looked like a pool, with a ledge running all the way round it. Above the ledge were smears of colour. They reminded him of something, though for a minute he couldn't think what it was. Then it came back to him. A cave – his captors had brought him through the undersea tunnel into a cave, with mirrors of rainbow colours set in a circle round it –

He was behind the yellow mirror!

Quickly, feeling his way, Kes explored

further along the wall. He soon realized that his suspicion was right – the wall curved round until it came back to the mirror again. He was imprisoned in a sphere of water, with no way out.

'Hey!' He hammered on the mirror with both fists, feeling angry now as well as frightened. 'Let me out!'

His hammering made no sound, and he felt sure that no one beyond the mirror could hear him. Where *was* this place? And where was his mother? Pressing his face to the transparent surface he tried again to get a clearer view, and this time he made out something, or someone, sitting on a rock at one side of the cave's central pool. He was sure that the figure hadn't been there a minute ago, and his pulse quickened as he recognized the familiar shape of a long shining tail.

'Mother?' he shouted. 'Mother!'

The shape moved. It *was* a mermaid, but

her hair was black, not gold. Kes's hope turned to alarm. Then the mermaid raised one hand and pointed towards him.

Instantly the clear wall dissolved. Suddenly freed, the whole weight of water behind it erupted outwards, carrying Kes with it, and he tumbled out of the mirror and into the pool.

Kes plunged under and down, thrown this way and that by the churning water. At last it calmed enough for him to right himself and he surfaced. As he gasped and shook his head in an effort to clear water from his eyes, a voice said, 'Welcome, Kesson. I am *very* pleased to meet you.'

The mermaid he had seen through the mirror was gazing down at him with a smile on her face. Black hair with a blue sheen cascaded over her shoulders, and her eyes were brilliant emerald green. Her face was very beautiful, but it was also cruel and spiteful. On her head was a golden circlet set with seven pearls. At the foot of her rock couch another pair of eyes stared too. Tullor was there, coiled round the rock. His mouth was open and he looked as if he were grinning.

Kes stared back at them both in horror. The thought flashed across his mind, *Tullor's an eel! How can he survive out of water?* but he had no time to do more than wonder before the mermaid spoke again.

'Well?' she demanded. 'Haven't you got anything to say for yourself?' She leaned forward and the look in her eyes made Kes shiver. '*Do you know who I am?*'

Kes did know and, trembling, managed to find his voice. 'You are . . . Taran . . .'

Tullor snarled ferociously. 'She is *Queen* Taran! Say "Your Majesty" when you dare to speak to her!'

'Be quiet, Tullor!' Taran raised a hand and the giant eel cringed. 'Kesson is very young, and no doubt his mother hasn't taught him manners.' She looked at her servant. 'You've done well and you will be rewarded, but now go. I want to talk to our new friend alone.'

Tullor slid off the rock into the pool. Kes shrank back, but the eel only gave him a cold, ominous glare before disappearing below the surface without a ripple.

With Tullor gone a little of Kes's courage crept back and he said, 'Where's my mother? What have you done with her?'

'She's safe and well, for now,' Taran replied carelessly. Then her expression changed. 'But if you want her to *stay* well, you must do as I tell you and answer my questions truthfully. Do you understand?'

Kes swallowed and nodded.

'Good. Then come out of the water, and sit beside me.'

It was the last thing Kes wanted to do, but he dared not argue. He tried to haul himself from the pool and onto the couch. It wasn't easy with his mer-tail, and Taran smiled as she watched his efforts.

'Why don't you change back into your human form?' she asked, amused. 'Oh, don't look so surprised. I know *all* about you and your twin sister, so there's no point in trying to hide what you are.'

Kes flushed crimson. He willed himself to change, and when at last he managed to climb out of the water he looked like an ordinary boy.

'That's better,' said Taran sweetly. 'Now, let us talk. Do you know why you've been brought here?'

He shook his head. 'No . . . Your Majesty.'

'It's very simple.' Suddenly Taran reached out and gripped his arm. Kes winced; she was amazingly strong. She stared into his face, and her voice turned from sweetness to venom as she hissed, 'I want the silver pearl!'

Kes started to shake with fear. 'Th-the . . . silver pearl . . .?' he echoed.

'Yes! Don't pretend that you don't understand. I know you do. Your sister has it, in the locket she wears. And you've seen it, haven't you? Morvyr revealed the secret to you and your sister.'

'No, Your Majesty –'

'Don't lie to me! I *know*!' Taran's voice rose shrilly, then with an effort she got herself under control again. 'I *will* have the silver pearl, Kesson. And you will help me to get it.'

Kes's mind was spinning. How did Taran know about the pearl in Lizzy's locket? There was only one possible answer. When Lizzy and Morvyr met for the first time, Morvyr had shown them the locket's secret compartment. They had seen the silver pearl, and had heard the strange, high-pitched singing note it gave off when the compartment was opened. Morvyr had closed it quickly. But if Taran's servants had been spying, they too might have heard the pearl sing.

'Let me show you something.' Taran took off her golden circlet and held it out. Her voice was sweet and reasonable again. 'This is my crown, Kesson. The crown of your rightful Queen. Look more closely. See?' She pointed to the pearls set round the circlet's edge. 'It's incomplete. There should be nine pearls, but two of them are missing.' She stared intimidatingly into his face. 'Do you know what happened to them?'

Again Kes swallowed and shook his head.

'They were stolen,' said Taran softly. 'And do you know who stole them?'

'N-no, Your Majesty . . .'

'Then I'll tell you. Your mother stole them.'

Kes's eyes widened. 'No! She wouldn't –'

'*Don't interrupt me!*' Taran snarled. 'Your mother, Morvyr, stole the silver and black pearls from my crown and hid them. And I want them back!' She stared at him again. 'You saw one of the pearls in your sister's locket, didn't you, Kesson?'

Her eyes seemed to bore through Kes's skull and reach to his innermost thoughts, and he felt an awful sense of power radiating from her mind. He dared not lie to her, and he whispered, 'I saw . . . *a* pearl. But I don't know anything about it.' He swallowed and added, 'Your Majesty . . .'

'What colour was it?'

Shaking like a jellyfish, Kes replied, 'S-silver . . .'

'And do you know where the black pearl is?'

For the first time in his life Kes thanked his lucky stars that Morvyr had been so secretive. If she had told him about the pearls and he had tried to hide what he knew from Taran, he was absolutely certain she would have known it. And he shuddered to think of what she might have done then.

'P-please, Your Majesty,' he stammered, 'I don't know anything about a black pearl. I've never even heard of it before.'

The Queen continued to stare at him for a few more seconds. Then abruptly she sat back on her couch. 'I see you're telling the truth,' she said. 'That's very wise of you. It all happened a long time ago, so I suppose you were too young to remember.' She turned her attention to the circlet, stroking it, and Kes thought quickly. He knew now why Taran wanted the pearl in Lizzy's locket so much. But it seemed there was a black pearl too – where was that? Did Morvyr know? Kes didn't believe for a moment that his mother had stolen the pearls, but he was sure she must know something about the missing black one.

Then with a shock the last words of the message Arhans had brought slammed into his mind. *The ninth one is safe with me.*

There were seven pearls in Taran's circlet, and two missing – which made nine. Was that what his father had meant? Did *he* have the black pearl?

Suddenly Kes knew that, at all costs, Taran must not find out about Jack Carrick's return. He would have to be desperately careful, and hope that she wouldn't ask him any questions about his father. But if she did and looked into his eyes the way she had done a few minutes ago . . .

'What are you thinking, Kesson?'

Kes jumped, and looked up. Taran had put the circlet back on her head and was regarding him with her cold green eyes. He looked away and said, 'I was wondering . . . what you're going to do with Mother and me.'

She smiled. 'Oh, I see. You're frightened, are you? Well, don't worry, I'm not going to hurt you. I would, if it suited me, but I have a better plan. Your mother is going to stay

here for a while, as my . . . guest.' The way
she said '*guest*' made Kes shudder inwardly.
'And you are going to carry out a little
errand for me. If you complete it, like an
obedient boy, I will set Morvyr free. But, if
you fail . . .' She uttered an unpleasant
laugh. 'Well, let's just say that your mother
will regret that very much.'

Kes's fear came surging to the surface
again and he cried, 'Where is she? I want to
see her!'

'Of course you do. And you shall.' She
turned and looked at the indigo mirror. Then
she raised one hand and pointed at it.

Kes expected the mirror's surface to
dissolve in a cascade of water as the yellow
one had done. Instead, though, it swirled and
an image appeared in it.

Morvyr was behind the mirror, trapped
inside as Kes had been. She drifted in the
water, her golden hair moving slowly like a
pale cloud around her head, and her tail

drifted too, as though she had no control over it.

Kes shouted, '*Mother!*' and Taran laughed again.

'She can't hear you. She is asleep, and will stay asleep until I decide to wake her. *If* I decide to. But that depends on you.'

Kes stared at Morvyr's limp figure, and an ache of desperate, helpless fury rose up in him so that he could hardly breathe.

Finding his voice with an effort, he said, 'What do you want me to do?'

Taran looked triumphant. 'As I said, I want you to carry out a little errand for me. It's quite simple. You will go to shore and find your sister, Tegenn. Tell her that your mother is a captive, and the price of her freedom is the silver pearl.'

With a last shred of defiance Kes said, 'What if she won't give it to me?'

'Then you must persuade her. Otherwise you will never see your mother again. And you don't want that, do you?' She paused. 'Answer me!'

'No, Your Majesty,' Kes whispered miserably.

Taran gave a soft, low chuckle. 'You're a clever boy, Kesson. You understand that you can't defy me. Now you must make your sister understand too. I'm sure you can do that.'

Kes knew that he had no choice. Slowly he nodded.

'When you have the pearl,' Taran went on, 'you will bring it here to me – and Tegenn must come with you.'

'But –'

'*Be quiet!* I want to meet her, so she must come! Then all three of you may go free.'

Could he believe that? Kes asked himself. Would Taran keep her word, or would she imprison them all? He didn't trust her . . . but if he didn't do what she wanted, she would hurt Morvyr.

Heart thumping, he said, 'All right. I'll bring her.'

'Good. Now, there's one more thing before I send you away to carry out your task. Each pearl has its own special gateway to the outside world, which it alone can unlock. You were brought here through the indigo gate, which I opened with the indigo pearl. However, you must bring the silver pearl through the silver gateway.' She smiled maliciously. 'No other pearl can unlock that portal. So, if you try to trick me, the gate will not open and I will know that the pearl is a fake.'

'How can I find the gateway?' Kes asked.

'Your snooping friends the dolphins know where all the gates are – much good may it do them!' said Taran scornfully. 'It's a long way from the land, so I'll give you time to do your task. But you *will* do it!'

Turning towards the pool, she clapped her hands sharply. Moments later the water churned and Tullor's head appeared above the surface.

'You summoned me, Your Majesty?' said the eel fawningly.

'Yes, Tullor. This boy is to return to the sea. Take him through the green gateway and let him go. And spread word that I am no longer searching for him; he is free to do as he pleases.'

'Your Majesty?' Tullor sounded surprised.

'Don't question me, Tullor! Just do as you're told!'

The eel ducked his head submissively. 'Of course, Your Majesty.' He glowered at Kes.

'Go, Kesson,' Taran ordered. 'And don't forget – if you try to deceive me, I'll know!'

Kes slipped off the rock and into the pool. Tullor swam round him, still glowering, and Taran held up the circlet. She touched the green pearl, which began to glow. The pool glowed too, and the water turned to the same emerald hue as the pearl. Then, so suddenly that Kes was taken completely by surprise, the water churned and swirled. Spinning round, he felt a powerful pull, and the next instant he and Tullor plunged under the surface and were sucked into what felt like a huge whirlpool. Down and round, twisting and whirling – colours flashed in front of Kes's eyes. He spun upside down, sideways, every way – then there was a *whoosh*ing sound, and he and the eel burst out of the tunnel and into the open sea.

Kes gasped dizzily and thrashed his arms and legs until he was – or thought he was – upright. Tullor had recovered more quickly, and his cold eyes were full of hate as he said, 'Her Majesty has told me you are to be left alone, and I obey. But if I had a choice . . .' He let the threat hang unfinished.

Kes tried to ignore it and looked around. Light was filtering down from above, which meant it must be day, but it was very dim. They were in deep sea, he realised, and nothing looked familiar. 'Where is this?' he demanded.

'Ask the dolphins,' Tullor retorted spitefully. 'They like to think they know everything. They'll tell you where you are – *if* you can find them.'

If the eel had been capable of laughing, Kes thought, he would have cackled aloud. Kes said nothing, and after a few moments Tullor hissed, 'I will see you again, Kesson. Be sure of that.'

He writhed round and swam away. Kes watched until he vanished in the undersea gloom, then breathed out a sigh of relief. He might be lost and alone, but anything was better than having Tullor for a companion. He would find his own way to land. Someone would tell him where he was. And maybe he would meet a friend who could get a message quickly to Arhans. He needed her now, as he had never done before.

Closing his eyes, he willed himself to

change from human to merboy. When the change was complete, he flicked his tail, feeling its strength. Then he stared into the endless, unfamiliar sea. It looked daunting. But he tried not to think about that.

'I'll bring the pearl back, Mother,' he whispered fiercely. 'I'll set you free. I promise!'

Bubbles streamed from his mouth and nose as he took a deep breath. Then he bunched his muscles and streaked away into the gloom.

FIND OUT MORE ABOUT

LOUISE COOPER

If you were a mermaid, what would you most like about it? And what would your mermaid name be?

I'd love to be able to talk to and understand all the other sea creatures and hear about their lives. And it would be wonderful to be able to cast a spell to make the sun shine! A name . . . well, I'd like something with a beautiful meaning, so I think I'd choose 'Sterganna', which in the Cornish language means *starlight*.

Are you a good swimmer like Lizzy?

I'm afraid not! I enjoy swimming, but I'm pretty hopeless at it. What I do love, though, is bodyboard-surfing at my local beach. That's really fun, but I'm always careful not to go out of my depth.

Do you have any brothers or sisters?

No, there's just me. My husband, Cas, is an only child too . . . but we do have a lovely cat!

Have you ever met anyone, or anything, as scary as Tullor?

Not THAT scary, I'm glad to say! I've seen conger eels in aquariums, and they're frightening enough behind glass! My friend's horse, Mischa, can be a bit scary, simply because she's so big; she's part thoroughbred and part shire, and seventeen hands high. But she's a gentle giant. You just have to watch where she puts her hoofs . . .

Have you ever swum with dolphins?

No – wouldn't it be wonderful? We see dolphins off the coast here in Cornwall, and when we went to the Isles of Scilly a group of them followed the ferry for about half an hour. My closest encounter was in Brittany: Cas and I were staying on a boat with some friends when, one evening, a dolphin came alongside and played and 'talked' to us. That was amazing, and something I'll always remember.

What was your favourite children's book?

No doubt about it, it's *The Lion, The Witch and The Wardrobe*. I first read it when I was about eight, and when I'd finished I tried to get into Narnia through the wardrobe in my parents' bedroom. I was desperately disappointed when it didn't work! For me, it's the most magical and exciting book ever and it still inspires me.

What do you like doing best of all?

My favourite thing of all is being by the sea and just enjoying it – fishing in rockpools, hunting for shells, making sandcastles, paddling or surfing, exploring, dreaming . . . I can't imagine anything nicer!

How did you become a writer?

When I was very young I was always inventing stories – usually spooky adventures – and I soon realized that a writer was the only thing I wanted to be. So I wrote and wrote and wrote, and sent my books to publishers until, at last, one was accepted. I've never looked back from there.

Visit Louise's official website at
louisecooper.com